# Autumn Whispers

## An Adventure Romance

### Harper St James

Harper St James Romance

Copyright © 2023 by Harper St James – All rights reserved.

In no way is it legal to reproduce, duplicate, or transmit any part of this document in either electronic means or in printed format. Recording of this publication is strictly prohibited and any storage of this document is not allowed unless written permission from the publisher.

All rights reserved.

Respective authors own all copyrights not held by the publisher.

# Contents

1. Chapter One — 1
2. Chapter Two — 8
3. Chapter Three — 15
4. Chapter Four — 22
5. Chapter Five — 28
6. Chapter Six — 35
7. Chapter Seven — 42
8. Chapter Eight — 48
9. Chapter Nine — 55
10. Chapter Ten — 62
11. Chapter Eleven — 69
12. Chapter Twelve — 76
13. Chapter Thirteen — 83
14. Chapter Fourteen — 90
15. Chapter Fifteen — 97
16. Chapter Sixteen — 104
17. Chapter Seventeen — 111

18. Chapter Eighteen — 117
19. Chapter Nineteen — 123
20. Chapter Twenty — 129
21. Chapter Twenty-One — 135
22. Chapter Twenty-Two — 141
23. Chapter Twenty-Three — 147
24. Chapter Twenty-Four — 153
25. Chapter Twenty-Five — 159
26. Chapter Twenty-Six — 165
27. Chapter Twenty-Seven — 171
28. Chapter Twenty-Eight — 177
29. Chapter Twenty-Nine — 183
30. Chapter Thirty — 190
31. Chapter Thirty-One — 196
32. The End — 202
33. Unlikely Alliances Sneak Peak — 204

# Chapter One

Sarah

Startled by a soft rapping coming from the direction of my boss's office door, my attention immediately moved in that direction.

"Sarah." David tilted his head back toward his office and walked back to his chair behind his desk, sitting down.

I leaned against the door jam. "Yes, sir?"

"Come in and shut the door."

"Yes, sir."

I stepped into David's office, feeling a knot of nervousness tightening in my stomach. I couldn't help but wonder why he had called me in. The last person he did that to… came back out looking a little pale. Good God, I didn't **think** I'd done anything wrong.

As I took a seat, my palms felt clammy, and my knees trembled slightly. David was a stern but fair supervisor. He looked up from his desk and met my gaze. He could sense my unease.

"Sarah," he began, his voice steady, "I want you to know that you haven't done anything wrong. This isn't about your job performance or any complaints."

A wave of relief washed over me, but I was still curious about why he called me in here.

David continued, "We've got some staffing issues next week. Between vacations, personal days, and the extra tours, we're short-handed. I know it's not ideal, but I need you to work with him during that time."

I nodded, absorbing the distressing news. David had told me that he would do what he could to always keep that jerk and me apart, and schedule us for different areas. I hoped I'd never even see him again, much less have to work with my ex-boyfriend again, especially considering the reason for our breakup.

Seeing the concern in my eyes, David softened his tone. "Sarah, I'm aware of the situation with your ex, and I'm sorry about that. But... there's a silver lining here. After that week, I want you to take some time off. I've arranged for you to visit Black Hills National Park in South Dakota. Don't your parents live near there?"

I blinked in surprise. I'd been wanting a chance to escape my current situation, and the prospect of exploring a new park was enticing. "Yes, sir. They live near Sioux Falls."

"This could be even an easier move for you than I thought."

"David, thank you. I appreciate that," I said with gratitude.

David leaned back in his chair, a knowing smile on his face. "I've talked to the park manager, Benjamin Walters, and there's a position that's going to open up soon. I've already enlisted my wife's help to gather information about the area for you. Consider it a scouting mission. If you like what you see, you can put in for a transfer. And just so you know, it would be a quick transfer. You might even be able to start the following week, but you'll need to discuss that with him."

I couldn't believe my ears. The opportunity to leave behind my past, along with the constant reminder of his betrayal, and start over in a new national park was more than I could have hoped for.

"Thank you, David," I said, my voice choked with emotion. "This means the world to me."

David nodded, understanding the importance of this chance for me. "As much as I don't want to lose you here, I know you need this. And you've earned it, Sarah. Take that week to recharge, clear your head, and decide if it's what you want. We'll sort out the details, and I'll make sure you're well-prepared for your visit there."

With a newfound sense of hope, I left David's office, my frazzled nerves had been replaced by anticipation of new beginnings that awaited me and the possibility of a fresh start far away from my ex-boyfriend.

• ♥ • ♥ • ♥ • ♥ • ♥ •

That had to be one of the worst weeks I'd had in a long time. Warren tried to act like nothing happened and even tried hitting on me a few times. Setting him straight, that he and I were no longer a couple, took too many attempts, all of which failed. By the end of the week, I was ready to call up my ex-friend, his heavily pregnant wife, and tell her just how much of a scum bag he really was, but then I thought, "Screw it! The two of them deserve each other."

The week mercifully and finally ended, and I began packing in earnest. While initially contemplating the idea of a road trip, the thought of enduring over twenty hours on the highway didn't sound like fun in the least. Consequently, I bought a plane ticket a few days after David told me about this opportunity. It would be so much easier, and definitely faster, to fly there and then just rent an SUV from a car rental company at the airport in Rapid City.

The day I had been eagerly awaiting arrived, and with my bags packed, I called an Uber to take me to the airport. The flight itself was blissfully boring, and once I left the airport terminal, I headed to the car rental counter, where I secured a spacious, full-size SUV.

The difference between the hot and muggy autumn of Texas and the cooler weather here was a Godsend. Plugging in the address to the Moose Creek Campground and RV Park, I rolled the window down and took off. The prospect of driving through the changing landscape filled me with anticipation.

My destination lay nestled near the breathtaking Black Hills National Forest. The vibrant autumn colors, in vivid hues of red and gold, greeted me like new friends.

At the check-in desk, I met a welcoming woman in her early sixties, her warm smile put me instantly at ease. She efficiently handled the paperwork and then kindly offered to accompany me to my cabin.

As we drove to the cabin, I marveled at the beauty of the landscape, which was so different from what I'd seen in the past six years. The crisp, clean air, the rustling leaves, and the sense of tranquility enveloped me. I knew I was in for a memorable stay.

"The Moose Creek Campground and RV Park is a picturesque haven nestled amid the captivating beauty of the Black Hills National Forest." Angie, the woman who had checked me in, began to describe the place as if she was reading off a script as we drove.

She went on to explain that the property boasted a total of 15 charming cabins, each tucked away amidst the lush greenery, offering a cozy and secluded retreat for guests seeking solitude. As we passed by, I could see some of them, their wooden exteriors blending charmingly with the natural surroundings.

I wondered about the more than fifty RV parking sites, and just how full this place would get. The exact number was too many to count, and I selfishly hoped no more would come. The park seemed vast. With the occasional RV nestled beneath the towering trees, and people enjoying the serenity of this place, my excitement grew.

Angie mentioned a building available for rent, perfect for hosting gatherings or parties. I imagined it as a welcoming space where guests could come together and celebrate amidst this picturesque setting.

She also mentioned a separate set of bathrooms for those who preferred camping in tents. Although it was a thoughtful addition, I wouldn't be needing those facilities; my cabin was equipped with a mini kitchen and a shower stall, providing all the comfort and convenience I would want during my stay.

As I stepped out of the SUV and looked around, I felt a sense of wonder and gratitude for having the opportunity to experience this tranquil slice of nature, complete with its cozy cabins, RV sites, the promise of serene days ahead, and the possibility of a new job and new life.

After getting settled into my peaceful cabin, the allure of the outdoors called to me. The tranquil surroundings beckoned, ensuring an adventure waiting to be found.

I slipped on a light jacket and decided to embark on a leisurely walk. The brisk autumn air filled my lungs with a sense of vitality as I set out. The aroma of fallen leaves infused the atmosphere with a comforting earthiness, and the woods whispered promises of exploration.

My curiosity led me in the opposite direction of the check-in office, and soon, I was strolling past some of the RV sites. Families and individuals had set up camp, and with a warm smile on my face, I greeted the friendly folks I encountered along the way.

I exchanged pleasantries with those sitting outside, under their RV's canopy, sharing a sense of companionship with fellow nature enthusiasts. Some were reading books, others were sipping coffee, and a few were simply basking in the peaceful ambiance of the campground.

As I strolled through the park, my attention was drawn to the last RV site. There, a sizeable RV stood. With the canopy out and chairs around, I wondered who was inside, and how many people were in that family.

I continued walking and neared the last RV. When I arrived, I was met with a friendly face. A man with a warm smile stood near the door. He appeared to be in his mid-thirties, with brown hair that was slightly tousled. He was an impressive 6'2" and had a muscular build that hinted at a commitment to physical fitness.

With a friendly smile, I greeted him, sparking a pleasant conversation about the surrounding natural beauty and the peaceful ambiance of the park. There was an air of warmth and approachability about him, and I found myself at ease in his presence.

"It's truly beautiful here, isn't it? My name's Sarah Riley, by the way."

"Absolutely, Sarah. I'm Hudson West," he replied, extending a hand in a firm handshake. "Nice to meet you. Is this your first time at this park?"

"Yes, it is. God, it's just... so beautiful here. I love it."

"I couldn't agree more," he said with a smile. "I've been managing this place for a while now, and I never get tired of it. So, what brings you to the park?"

"Well," I hesitated. "I heard about the natural beauty of this area and thought it was time for a change of scenery and possibly a new job. I've lived in South Dakota before, but I've never been to the national park."

"Then you've missed out, but a change of scenery can work wonders," he said, nodding in understanding. "I hope you find what you're looking for here. If you need any tips or recommendations, feel free to ask."

"Thanks, Hudson. I appreciate that."

Our conversation continued, filled with shared stories and laughter, as the sun began to dip below the horizon. In Hudson's company, the tranquility of the park felt even more inviting.

"Well, it's been great meeting you Hudson, but I'm going back to my cabin. I hope you have a good night."

"I'm glad you decided to take a walk and stop to talk with me. It's been good meeting you as well. If you have any problems with the cabin, just let me know. The office closed about half an hour ago."

"Good to know. Well... good night."

I made my way back to my cabin. The night had settled in, creating a serene calm over the park. The moonlight filtered through the trees, casting gentle shadows on the path before me.

As I entered my cabin and settled in, my thoughts drifted back to Hudson. His warm smile, his easygoing demeanor, and his striking appearance all lingered in my mind. It was as if a magnetic pull had connected me to him during our brief encounter.

I replayed our conversation, relishing the moments we shared. It wasn't just his good looks that captivated me; it was the way he made me feel. In his presence, I felt a sense of comfort that I hadn't experienced in a long time.

I couldn't deny the flutter of excitement in my chest as I entertained the idea of seeing him again. The night air seemed to whisper sweet secrets of possibilities, and I drifted off to sleep with the image of his warm smile etched in my mind.

# Chapter Two

### Sarah

The most difficult part of applying for new jobs in the park system lies in the dreaded resume. Instead of the succinct bullet points that encapsulate each role you've undertaken, the National Park Service insists on comprehensive paragraphs replete with intricate details. Fortunately, I had diligently maintained mine, documenting the array of responsibilities I'd taken part in during my six-year tenure.

Armed with my meticulously updated resume, I embarked on my trip to the Hell Canyon Ranger District in Custer, with the early morning sun as my companion. My intent was to engage in a face-to-face conversation with Benjamin Walters, the Forest Supervisor at that location. This way, I hoped to gain deeper insights into the upcoming job opportunity. Even back in Texas, I had taken the initiative to arrange an appointment for this discussion.

"So, you're Sarah Riley," Mr. Walters remarked with a congenial smile. "David's filled me in on some of your background and your desire for a change of scenery. I trust you've brought your resume. It would certainly aid me in assessing your qualifications for the position. David did express his reluctance to see you go, but he's also committed to assisting you in this."

"Yes, sir," I replied, offering my resume to him. There wasn't much else to add. Just thinking about what happened still makes me angry.

He delved into the pages of my resume, his brows occasionally furrowing in contemplation, while sporadic affirmations of "Uh huh" and "That's good" escaped his lips. Finally, when he had perused every detail, he looked up, offering a reassuring smile.

"You possess quite a few of the qualifications we need," he affirmed. "I believe you would be an excellent fit for the position. I'll have to call David and let him know that he's going to lose a valuable asset if I have anything to say about it, and I do."

Relief washed over me like a soothing wave, and my smile beamed. I knew it wouldn't be as easy as that, but my chances of changing locations just shot up so much further than if I'd done this on my own.

"You know how this works. You'll need to apply for the position online and as soon as I get the notification, I'll call you and let you know. The sooner you apply, the sooner you can start."

"Thank you, Mr. Walters. I really appreciate this. I'll take care of that as soon as I get back to my cabin." I felt the grin on my face as if it were set in stone.

The drive back was a blissful one, and my smile was firmly etched on my face, an expression that seemed impossible to erase. As soon as I parked in front of the cabin, I practically leaped out of the SUV and made a beeline for the door. My fingers flew over the keyboard as I promptly submitted my request to change parks, the anticipation building with every click.

Within mere minutes, my phone rang, and I eagerly answered. It was incredible how connections between people could wield such influence... and so quickly too.

As I hung up the phone, a euphoric burst of laughter escaped my lips, replacing my smile with unbridled joy. Mr. Walters had worked his magic by swiftly informing David about my successful job transition. It meant that, after this brief vacation, I would only be working at Angelina National Forest for one more week. The prospect of genuinely enjoying this time away, free from any worries, washed over me, and I felt a renewed sense of liberation. I was determined to make the most of this fresh start.

No matter what that cheating, lying, piece of... ahem... "he" might say or do when I got back to Angelina, I highly doubted that anything he says or does, will matter to me... ever again.

When someone knocked on the door, I nearly jumped out of my skin, and I had to laugh at myself. My heart sped up and when I opened the door, Hudson stood there with a worried furrow on his brow.

"Uh... I was walking by and heard someone scream. Are you all right?" he inquired, the concern was evident in his voice and demeanor.

For some inexplicable reason, laughter bubbled up from deep within me, and the worried expression on Hudson's face shifted into one of amusement.

"I just found out that I got the job!" I practically shouted amid my almost uncontrollable joy. It was a feeling of happiness I hadn't experienced in far too long.

"Job?" he asked, clearly intrigued. "You mean the job you were applying for... **today**?"

"I'll be transferring from Angelina to here in just two weeks!" I exclaimed, so caught up in the joy of the moment that I couldn't contain my enthusiasm. I practically danced on the spot before impulsively hugging Hudson, my joy getting the best of me.

I quickly stepped back, a flush of embarrassment coloring my cheeks. "Oh my gosh! I'm so sorry," I apologized, my laughter now mingled with awkwardness even though he hugged me back.

Now it was Hudson's turn to chuckle. "Congratulations, and don't worry about it," he reassured me with a warm smile.

"Oh my gosh!" I exclaimed, my excitement giving way to a sudden rush of anxiety. "There's so much I need to do. I have to head back to the park, speak with Mr. Walters, and figure out whether I can stay in ranger housing or if I'll need to find something outside the park. Oh gosh!" I gasped, covering my mouth with my hand as my heart raced and dizziness set in.

"Whoa, whoa, whoa. Take a seat," Hudson urged, concern covering his face. "You're looking a bit pale. Let me grab you some water or, if you prefer, a shot of whiskey. If you don't have any, I do."

Hudson's comforting presence was like a lifeline as I sank into a chair, feeling the anxiety and excitement collide within me. His warm smile and reassuring words helped ease the initial shock of my impending transfer.

"Thanks," I murmured, taking a deep breath to steady my racing heart. "I can't believe it, but it's a bit overwhelming."

Hudson leaned in, his voice a soothing balm. "Take your time. It's a big change, but you've got this. But is something bothering you? You were so excited and then…"

As I began to share my story about my ex, the hurt and betrayal I'd experienced flowed out of me. Hudson listened attentively, his empathy a comforting anchor in the storm of emotions.

"It's been a tough road," I admitted, my voice trembling. "That's why I'm making this move, but I can't help feeling nervous about all the details I need to sort out."

Hudson's eyes were filled with understanding. "I'm here to help in any way I can. And to celebrate this new chapter, how about we go for a hike to my favorite spot in the park? It will calm your nerves and you can see some of the park."

The thought of immersing myself in nature, away from the chaos of my life, sounded like a perfect remedy. I nodded in agreement. "That sounds great."

Before we set off on our adventure, I decided to make a call to Mr. Walters to express my gratitude and clarify some details. After a brief conversation, I hung up the phone with a smile.

"I can stay in ranger housing," I informed Hudson. "That's one less thing to worry about."

As we readied ourselves for the hike to Jewel Cave National Monument, a sense of renewed energy coursed through me. Hudson's company and the prospect of immersing myself in the wonders of nature filled me with anticipation. It wasn't an ending; it was the beginning of a new chapter, and I faced it with hope and determination, bolstered by the support of a newfound friend.

The afternoon sunbathed the rugged landscape in warm, golden light as Hudson and I set out on our hike to Jewel Cave. The air was comfortably mild, carrying the invigorating scent of the pine trees that surrounded us, reaching for the sky, like ancient guardians of the forest.

Hudson led the way with a confident stride, and I followed, entranced by the natural beauty that enveloped us. The forest was dominated by the changing colors of the aspen, birch, and maple trees. Brilliant shades of yellow, gold, and red. It was as if the earth itself had decided to put on a show.

The towering pines whispered secrets to the clear blue sky, their branches swaying gently in the breeze. The forest was alive with the melodious songs of birds, their tunes echoing through the tall trees. Squirrels chattered and scampered, their antics providing a playful backdrop to the woodland symphony.

Our conversation flowed effortlessly, filled with our shared love for the great outdoors. We swapped stories of our favorite trails, and we recounted memorable encounters with wildlife. Amidst the serenity of nature, there were moments of comfortable silence, during which we simply absorbed the peacefulness that surrounded us.

Every now and then, I caught Hudson stealing glances in my direction, and a subtle warmth spread through me. That unspoken connection between us, that magnetic pull that had drawn me to him, maybe was drawing him to me as well. Though we'd only met yesterday, that connection hung in the air, like the scent of pine on a breeze. As we walked and talked, my heart felt light, and I couldn't help but steal glances at him too.

However, my moment of bliss was abruptly shattered when my foot slipped on a loose stone, and I stumbled, my ankle twisting with a sharp, shooting pain. I winced and let out a soft cry, grabbing onto a nearby tree for support.

"Ow, ow, ow, ow!" I gasped, sucking in a breath between clenched teeth.

Hudson was by my side in an instant, his concern etched across his face. "Are you okay, Sarah?"

"I swear, you just can't take some people anywhere!" I said laughing through the pain and trying to cover my embarrassment.

I tried to put weight on my injured ankle, and while it hurt to do so, I could still move it. "I think I just twisted my ankle, nothing broken. It'll be fine." I admitted, my frustration was evident.

Hudson's strong arm encircled me. He supported my weight as we began the slow journey back toward his truck, which was parked quite a distance away. The hike back wasn't quick, but Hudson's presence was reassuring.

"Lean on me," he said, his voice soothing. "We'll get you back to the truck, and then we can take a closer look at that ankle."

Having Hudson's arm around me as we hobbled back along the trail provided an unexpected sense of comfort and security. His strong, reassuring presence radiated warmth that eased the discomfort in my twisted ankle. The gentle pressure of his arm supporting me made me feel safe and cared for. And until that moment, I didn't realize how much I'd missed feeling that way.

I nodded, grateful for his support. Despite the discomfort, I was fairly certain it was just a strain and would only require some ice. As we hobbled along, our conversation shifted to my well-being.

"It's not too far now," he reassured me as we approached the trailhead. "We'll get you patched up, and then we can still enjoy some time in the park."

I smiled through the pain. Hudson's presence made everything feel better or at least not as bad. With each step we took, his closeness became a source of calmness, and I found myself leaning into his strength. I enjoyed being held by him more than I wanted to admit.

We finally reached a rustic picnic area along the trail, and with Hudson's support, I gingerly lowered myself onto the weathered wooden seat at one of the tables. The pain in my twisted ankle was a constant reminder of my divided attention. I should have known better.

Hudson knelt beside me, concern showed in his eyes as he gently removed my shoe and sock, revealing my swollen and bruised ankle. I winced at the sight as the throbbing sensation intensified.

"That looks painful," he commented, his tone laced with concern.

I mustered a weak smile despite the discomfort. "I should've brought hiking boots instead of just these sneakers," I quipped, my voice tinged with self-recrimination. "But thank God it's my left foot, at least I can still drive. There goes my plans to explore the park while I'm here."

Hudson chuckled softly, his fingers tenderly assessing the extent of the injury. His touch was gentle, and even in this less-than-ideal situation, there was a sense of intimacy between us that I couldn't ignore as his fingers lingered on my skin for longer than necessary.

# Chapter Three

Hudson

"You never know," I said, offering a glimmer of hope. "By tomorrow, the swelling could go down significantly and not completely spoil your plans to explore the park."

Her response was a mixture of optimism and determination. "I don't know, but I like that positive attitude. I think we should just go back to the campground, and I'll ice it... all night if I have to."

Seeing her smile light up with the possibility of a quick recovery was a sight to behold. Her long, brown hair was neatly tied up in a ponytail, accentuating her natural beauty. As I knelt there, I found myself wondering about her age and if I was too old for her. I hoped our age difference, and I knew there was one, wouldn't be a concern for her. It was a fleeting, slightly depressing thought, and unfortunately, I showed that emotion for her to see.

Her beautiful brown eyes, filled with worry, caught me off guard. "What's wrong?" she asked, her genuine concern surprising me.

I hesitated for a moment, my nerves getting the best of me. "Oh, it's nothing," I replied, attempting to downplay my feelings. "I was just hoping your plans don't get completely messed up."

In truth, I wanted to say so much more, to express how much I enjoyed her company and how I wanted to spend more time with her to get to know her better. But the words remained unspoken, buried beneath my uncertainty.

"I don't know how you'd feel about this," I began, carefully choosing my words, "but if it's too much for you to walk, I can carry you."

Her initial response was hesitant. "Really? I mean... I don't want to impose. You've already gone above and beyond for me."

I wanted to reassure her, to make it clear that offering to help was not a burden. "Really," I insisted. "It's absolutely fine. I wouldn't have offered if I thought I would be inconvenienced by it."

Her laughter, pure and genuine, was like music to my ears. "It's been a while since I've had a piggyback ride," she admitted with a playful grin. "I just don't want to be seen by any of the rangers. It would be too embarrassing," she confessed.

I understood her concern and wanted to put her at ease. "If I spot one of them, you can simply hide your face until I give you the all-clear," I offered, hoping to alleviate any worry she might have about being seen. And I wanted to carry her, to see what she felt like against my body.

As gently as possible, I helped Sarah slide her sock and shoe back onto her foot. I couldn't help but notice the vulnerability in her eyes, mixed with gratitude. There was something undeniably intimate about this simple act, a moment that seemed to draw us closer.

Once her shoe was on, she shifted her weight, ready to climb onto my back. I positioned myself to make it as easy as possible for her. She wrapped her arms around my shoulders and settled onto my back, locking her legs around my hips. I felt a sense of protectiveness, chivalry, and attraction, plus I wanted to be close to her.

Her weight was unsurprisingly easy to bear as I stood and began the trip back to my truck. I kept my eyes on the trail ahead, and after a short distance, I spotted a ranger approaching. Knowing she would start working here soon, I knew Sarah didn't want to be seen in this situation, so I gently leaned closer to her ear and whispered, "Ranger coming. Just stay low and you'll be fine."

As the ranger drew nearer, he noticed us and called out, "Hey there, folks. Is everything all right?"

Sarah, on my back, held her breath for a moment, and I felt her grip on my shoulders tighten. She quickly ducked her head, effectively hiding her face.

I greeted the ranger with a friendly nod. "Yeah, just taking a little breather here. She's got me working hard, you know. I'm practically her humble servant," I quipped with a playful tone, trying to keep the mood light.

The ranger seemed satisfied with the explanation and offered a warm smile. "All right, take care," he gave me a thumbs up. "If you need any help, just let us know."

He continued on his way, and I could feel Sarah relax behind me. She raised her head and whispered, "Thanks for that, but seriously… humble servant, huh?"

A chuckle bubbled up as I glanced over my shoulder at her. "No problem. Your wish is my command." I hoped it wasn't just my imagination, but I couldn't deny the sense of closeness that I felt for her. I knew I felt it, but did she?

• ♥ • ♥ • ♥ • ♥ • ♥ •

I made a quick stop at the campground's clubhouse to grab a zip bag, some ice, and a towel. Sarah had been a trooper, but her ankle needed attention and I was determined to help.

We returned to the cabin, and I could see that she was in pain, and her face was drawn with discomfort. She sat on the edge of the bed while I set the items down on a nearby table.

Carefully, I knelt in front of her and began to remove her shoe and sock once more. My heart sank as I noticed that her ankle had swelled further, and the bruising had grown, encompassing a much larger part of her foot.

"Does it hurt more?" I asked, my voice filled with concern as I gently examined her injury.

Sarah's words caught me by surprise. "It hurts when you touch it, but it also feels good," she admitted with a sheepish grin.

I chuckled at her candidness. "Well, I'll try to be as gentle as possible," I replied, my fingers continuing their careful examination of her swollen ankle.

As I applied the ice pack wrapped in the towel to her injury, she winced but then sighed in relief. "That's better," she whispered, closing her eyes briefly.

"I'm glad it's helping," I said softly, watching her closely for any signs of discomfort. "You'll need to keep it elevated and iced for a while. It should help with the swelling."

Sarah nodded and leaned back, propping her injured ankle on a couple of pillows. Her expression shifted from one of pain to one of gratitude. "Thanks for taking care of me, Hudson. You didn't have to do all this."

I smiled at her warmly. "I wanted to. Besides, it's the least I can do after giving you a piggyback ride."

As I sat there watching her, I couldn't ignore the connection that had been growing between us. It was like an unspoken bond, and I found myself wanting to get to know her even better. There was something about her that drew me in, something beyond her physical beauty, which was undeniable.

We fell into a comfortable silence, the only sound in the room was the soft hum of the small refrigerator. I continued to hold the ice pack against her ankle, my fingers lightly brushing her skin. It was an intimate moment, and I felt a sense of closeness to her that I didn't understand.

Sarah eventually broke the silence. "So, tell me more about yourself, Hudson. What brought you to this park, and how did you end up as the manager?"

I leaned back in my chair, giving her a thoughtful look. "Well, I've always had a love for the outdoors, for nature. I grew up in a small town near here, and my family spent a lot of time exploring the Black Hills. After college, I knew I wanted to work in a place like this, so I bought the land and created this RV park."

Sarah's eyes sparkled with interest as she listened. "That's amazing. It sounds like you're living your dream."

I nodded, a sense of contentment washing over me. "I am, and as for how I came to own and manage this place, it was a combination of hard work and good timing. I saw the potential in this land and decided to turn it into an RV park. It's been a labor of love, and I couldn't be happier with how it's turned out."

Sarah smiled, her eyes never leaving mine. "It's clear that you love what you do. I can see the passion in your eyes when you talk about this place."

Her words warmed my heart, and I was drawn even closer to her. "I do love it here. But enough about me. Tell me more about your plans, Sarah. What do you hope to do when you start working here?"

Sarah's face lit up with excitement as she began to share her aspirations. She talked about her experience at Angelina National Forest, her desire to continue working in a park setting, and her hope to make a positive impact on the area and the visitors who came here. It was clear that she had a deep passion for her work.

Listening to her talk, I admired her dedication and enthusiasm. She had faced challenges and setbacks, but she was determined to move forward and make the most of this fresh start.

As our conversation continued, I found myself opening up to her in a way I hadn't with anyone else in a long time. It was easy to talk to her and to share my thoughts and dreams. The connection between us was undeniable, and it was growing stronger with each passing moment.

"I'll get some more ice for you. I'll be back in a few minutes." Quickly running to the clubhouse and returning, I removed the ice pack from her ankle and replaced it with a new one.

*Sarah*

Hudson gently placed the ice pack on my ankle and the cold sensation brought immediate relief to the throbbing pain. I sighed with gratitude as he adjusted the ice pack, making sure it was in the right position. Now, if it reduces the swelling, I'll be so much happier.

Eventually, the evening sun began to cast long shadows in the room, signaling the approach of night. "I should let you get some rest," he said reluctantly.

I nodded, a look of gratitude in my eyes. "Thank you, Hudson. You've been amazing. I appreciate everything you've done for me."

He leaned in closer, his voice soft and sincere. "It's my pleasure. Get some rest, and if you need anything, don't hesitate to ask." He wrote something on the notepad on the table. "This is my number. Call me if you need anything."

He made his way to the door, and I felt a sense of longing. There was something special about him, something that had touched my heart in a way I hadn't expected.

I settled back on the bed with my injured ankle elevated and the ice pack in place. I felt grateful for Hudson's presence and care. Despite the unexpected twist in my plans, I found comfort in the fact that I wasn't alone in having to deal with a sprained ankle. And maybe, just maybe, there was something more between us than just a chance encounter.

We'd spent the entire evening sharing and getting to know each other better. After what happened with Warren, I didn't think I'd ever look at another man again. But there was something magnetic about Hudson.

My thoughts continued to focus completely on Hudson. He was unlike anyone I'd ever met. His passion for this place, his determination, and the way his eyes lit up when he talked about it were captivating. But it was more than that. There was a warmth in his smile, a genuine kindness in his actions that made me feel safe, something I hadn't felt in a long time.

I wondered about the man behind the rugged exterior. What had shaped him into the person he was today? And why did I feel such a strong connection to him, as if fate had brought us together at this moment?

Despite the pain in my ankle and the turmoil of recent events, being here with Hudson felt like a ray of hope in the darkness. I knew I was far from healed, both physically and emotionally, but there was something about his presence that made me believe that I might be able to find happiness and peace again.

# Chapter Four

### Sarah

I woke up the next morning with a dull ache in my ankle. Gently, I propped myself up on my elbows and glanced down at the injury. Some of the swelling had subsided overnight, but it was far from fully healed. The bruise had darkened, taking on an ominous shade of purple, but it didn't hurt as much as I expected.

As I carefully moved my foot, testing its mobility, I realized that the pain was manageable, thanks in no small part to Hudson's care the previous evening. His soothing presence and expert handling of my injury had made a significant difference.

Just as I was contemplating getting up to find some more ice for my ankle, I heard a knock at the door. Surprised, I called out, "I'm coming!" and quickly swung my legs over the edge of the bed. I didn't expect anyone at this early hour, and curiosity piqued my interest.

When I opened the door, there he was, Hudson, standing on the porch with a warm smile. My heart skipped a beat at the sight of him. He had been the only thing on my mind since he left the room last night.

"Morning," he greeted me, his voice warm and friendly.

"Good morning," I replied, trying to hide the blush that crept onto my cheeks. It wasn't just his rugged charm but also his genuine concern that made my heart flutter.

Hudson glanced down at my ankle. Feeling self-conscious about the state of my injury, I looked down.

"How's your ankle feeling today?" he asked, the concern evident in his eyes and voice.

"It's better, thanks to your help yesterday," I admitted, offering a shy smile. "I was just about to get some more ice for it."

Hudson nodded, and without a word, he reached down and picked up a small cooler filled with ice packs. It was as if he had anticipated my needs.

"Here you go," he said, handing me one of the ice packs. "Keep using these. It should help with the swelling."

I took the ice pack with gratitude, our fingers brushing for a brief moment. His touch sent a shiver down my spine, and I was drawn to his gaze. In that instant, I knew there was something special between us. It wasn't just me letting my imagination run wild. The connection went beyond my injury.

"Thank you," I said sincerely. "You've been so kind."

His smile widened, and there was a warmth in his eyes that made my heart race. "It's my pleasure. I just want to make sure you're comfortable and well taken care of."

Hudson left to tend to his duties, and I closed the door behind me. I couldn't shake the feeling that meeting him was a turning point in my life. Despite the circumstances that had brought me here, I felt a glimmer of hope for the future, all because of the man who had become my unexpected lifeline in this unfamiliar place.

I'd been lying in bed for what felt like an eternity, my laptop perched on my thighs as I balanced an ice pack on my still-tender ankle. Surfing the web and exchanging emails with David, my boss, had been a big help to me. I was fortunate that I currently lived in ranger housing, which meant I only needed to pack clothes and a few keepsakes when I moved in a couple of weeks.

One email caught my attention, and it made me smile. It was from Mr. Walters, my new boss, requesting my pants and shirt sizes. That meant my journey into the world of the

Black Hills National Park was inching closer. Feeling a mix of excitement and restlessness, I replied with my sizes and a note telling him I was looking forward to working with him.

Just as I was wondering what to do next, the unmistakable aroma of barbecue wafted into the room, tantalizing my senses. My stomach growled in response, and I couldn't believe my ears when I heard a knock on the door.

"Coming!" I called out, hastily closing my laptop and placing it on the bedside table. With a newfound burst of energy, I hobbled to the door and opened it, a grin spreading across my face at the sight before me. Hudson, that incredible man, who had taken such good care of me, was at it again.

He stood there holding a tray with a barbecue sandwich, a bag of chips, and a drink that looked like tea. The meal was perfect. Exactly what I was craving after smelling it. Barbeque was my favorite. My eyes widened in surprise and delight.

"Wow, Hudson, you've got impeccable timing," I exclaimed, my mouth practically watering at the delicious meal he had brought. "I was just about to whip up something for lunch, but this looks way better."

Hudson chuckled, his eyes twinkling with amusement. "Well, I couldn't let you suffer through another sandwich-making session. Besides, I've got a reputation to uphold as the best barbecue sandwich delivery guy in town."

I had to laugh at his playful tone. "You're certainly living up to that reputation. Thanks for being my personal delivery guy today."

He handed me the tray, and I balanced it carefully as I moved back into the room. Hudson followed me inside, and we settled into a comfortable conversation as I dug into the delicious barbecue sandwich.

The first bite sent waves of pure delight coursing through me, and an involuntary moan escaped my mouth. It was, without a doubt, the most exquisite barbeque sandwich I'd ever had the pleasure of eating. As I savored each succulent morsel, a sense of complete relaxation washed over me, causing my posture to slump in sheer contentment. I couldn't help but moan again, unable to contain my satisfaction.

"Oh my God!" I exclaimed between bites, my taste buds in blissful delight. "This is beyond amazing. Did you cook this?"

Hudson laughed, a mischievous glint in his eye as he replied, "Yes, I started it last night and thought you might like some. From all the sounds you're making, I'm guessing you really like it. Give me a second. Let me just start taking some notes here. Barbeque, check. Unsweet tea, check. Plain potato chips, check. Anything else I'm missing?" he stated as he wrote in the air.

His playful banter only added to his charm, but he looked more than pleased with himself and the smile that covered his face made him even more attractive to me.

As I took another bite, Hudson pointed to the corner of his mouth and made little circles "You've ah... got a little..." Picking up a paper napkin, he reached over to wipe the barbeque from the side of my mouth.

I swallowed hard, and my heart fluttered. "Yep, you just can't take some people anywhere."

"So, how's your ankle feeling today?" he asked with genuine concern in his voice.

I took a bite, savoring the rich flavors dancing on my taste buds, and answered with a playful smirk, "It may not look like it, but it's much better after all the ice, and now that I have this amazing barbecue to distract me."

Hudson's chuckle was infectious, and for a moment, it felt like we were old friends. "Glad I could be of service in more ways than one," he quipped with a twinkle in his eyes.

When Hudson asked about my plans for the day, I frowned as I glanced at my still slightly swollen ankle. "Well," I began hesitantly, "I did find a store in Custer that sells hiking boots. I was thinking of heading there today."

However, speaking with the voice of reason, Hudson gently advised, "Sarah, I understand your eagerness to get back out there, but waiting one more day is probably for the best. Let that swelling go down further. It'll be worth it in the long run."

I sighed in frustration, the walls of my cozy cabin felt like they were closing in on me. "I get it, but I'm going stir-crazy in here even though I can see the outside. I really hope that

that makes sense. The thing is, I need the outdoors. It's what I live for. It's why I became a park ranger. And it's so boring sitting here doing nothing," I whined like a toddler who didn't get her way.

I constantly felt a strong yearning for the open trails and the whisper of the wind through the trees. The forest called to me, and I was itching to explore its beauty. Reluctantly, I nodded. "Fine, but tomorrow I'm going! One more day of confinement and I'm out of here."

As the night settled in and the cabin grew dimmer, I felt an irresistible pull toward Hudson. Our conversations had evolved into something more, more intimate, more giving, and… just more. Hudson revealed himself to be not just intelligent and kind-hearted but also remarkably resilient and determined.

Hudson opened up about his role as the owner of the campground and RV park, expressing his deep affection for the Black Hills' natural beauty and his enthusiasm for ensuring guests enjoyed their stay. With every passing moment, the pull toward each other deepened, and I couldn't ignore the growing attraction I felt for him.

Chuckling, I recounted a comical incident from my previous job, and the cabin was filled with our laughter. Hudson's joy in seeing me happy was evident, and I was utterly captivated by his presence.

As the evening wore on, the realization that we were alone in the cabin became impossible to ignore. The lamp's soft glow cast a warm and inviting ambiance in the room, emphasizing the undeniable chemistry between us. My voice lowered as I shared a personal story from my past, one that had shaped me into the strong person I've become. Hudson's gentle touch, as he brushed a strand of hair from my face, made my heart flutter.

Our eyes met, and the unspoken bond between us grew stronger. It was as if fate itself conspired to bring us even closer together. Nothing else seemed to matter except the man sitting across from me.

I reached out my hand, touching his, feeling the warmth of his skin against mine. The desire to lean closer was overwhelming. I couldn't stop myself and our lips met in a tender, cautious kiss. It was a moment charged with longing and the excitement of new possibilities.

The kiss deepened, and the spark of desire flared between us. It was a collision of emotions and passion, a moment that felt like destiny unfolding before us.

When our lips met in that kiss, the world around me seemed to fade into insignificance. It was an instant, intense desire that burned like a bonfire between us. But just as things were heating up, a sound pierced the air, jolting us both back to reality.

I pulled away from Hudson, breathless and wide-eyed, my heart racing. Hudson's gaze was equally startled as we both turned to identify the source of the disturbance. It was the unmistakable sound of a car horn drawing nearer by the second.

I quickly glanced out of the window, spotting the headlights of a vehicle moving its way up the gravel road toward the cabin. Panic fluttered in my chest as I realized we had an unexpected visitor. I hastily adjusted my disheveled appearance, trying to regain my composure. Hudson and I exchanged a knowing glance as we separated.

The car eventually pulled up outside the cabin next to mine, and the engine shut off. We could hear laughter and the excited chatter of the newcomers. It seemed like I was about to have a new neighbor, and it was clear that our time had come to an end, at least for now.

A strange combination of relief and disappointment welled up inside me. Whatever was going on between us, made me want to explore it further. However, the unexpected arrival had thrown a curveball into the mix and disrupted our evening. It was as if fate had intervened, forcing us to put our desires on hold.

# Chapter Five

### Hudson

I knew my brother, James, and his girlfriend were arriving today. They'd been planning this visit for a while, and I'd been looking forward to catching up with him and meeting his new girlfriend. As I stepped out of the cabin, their nearby car was bathed in the cool, evening moonlight, and the sound of their animated voices drifted on the breeze as they unpacked their things.

With a welcoming smile, I made my way over to greet them. "Hey there, you two!" I greeted James with a hearty hug. "Glad you could make it. How was the drive?"

James grinned, his eyes sparkling with the familiarity of our close family. "Long, but we're finally here."

James introduced his girlfriend, Tammy, and while her handshake was probably meant as a friendly gesture, it lasted way longer than necessary. "I'm Tammy, by the way," she said, her overly sweet voice betraying her calculating eyes. "It's so nice to finally meet you, Hudson. James has told me so much about you."

I turned to Sarah, who had been quietly observing the exchange. "Likewise, Tammy. This is Sarah," I said, gesturing toward her. She offered a polite but strained smile. "She'll be your neighbor here at the campground."

Tammy's gaze shifted briefly to Sarah, and there was something in the way she looked at her, an air of superiority mixed with a touch of disdain. "Nice to meet you, Sarah," she replied, her tone a bit too condescending for comfort.

Sarah nodded, her jaw tight, and her breath noticeably faster. The tension surrounding her was unmistakable, and it was evident that there was more beneath the surface of Sarah's reaction. I couldn't be certain what caused a reaction like that, but the one thing I was certain of was that Sarah looked almost furious.

I invited James, Tammy, and Sarah to my RV to get better acquainted. Tammy hooked her arms with both James and me. Her gaze then shifted to Sarah as she asked if she was coming, not waiting for an answer before starting to walk, practically dragging both James and me along.

I felt uncomfortable with Tammy's overly familiar gesture, so I discreetly disengaged myself from her grip. It just didn't feel right. I walked back to Sarah, who was standing nearby, and asked if she wanted to come with us.

Sarah's angry expression concerned me. She shook her head and gave me a warning glance. "No, thanks. You go ahead... but I'd be careful around that Tammy too if I was you." She turned and walked into her cabin, leaving me standing there, looking at the closed door.

"What the heck does 'That Tammy too' mean?" I muttered under my breath, perplexed by Sarah's strange choice of words.

"Hey Bro! Come on, the party's just getting started." James yelled back to me as he and Tammy continued toward my RV.

I hesitated for a moment and then headed to my RV. Whatever was going on with Sarah, it could wait for now.

Once we settled inside my motor home, James, Tammy, and I popped open some beers and started catching up. It had been a while since I'd seen my brother, and I was genuinely happy to hear about what he'd been up to lately. The initial atmosphere was light-hearted, filled with jokes and laughter as we talked about our lives since we last saw each other.

Tammy seemed to fit right in with our banter. She had a good sense of humor and joined in the fun, making us laugh with her witty comments. We were having a good time, and I started to relax, thinking that maybe my initial unease was unwarranted.

However, as the evening wore on and the alcohol flowed more freely, Tammy's behavior took a turn for the worse. She sat uncomfortably close to me, her thigh pressing against mine, and she took every opportunity to touch my arm or shoulder. At one point, she even put her arm around me in a way that was far too close for my comfort.

James noticed her actions and grew increasingly agitated. I exchanged worried glances with him, and it was clear that he was not thrilled with how close Tammy was getting to me. The situation became even more uncomfortable as Tammy's flirting escalated.

Then, without warning, James abruptly stood up, his face flushed with anger. Without saying a word, he stormed out of the RV, leaving me and Tammy in an awkward and tense silence.

Tammy, realizing the consequences of her actions, hesitated for a moment. Then, with a conflicted expression, she got up and hurried after James, leaving me alone in the RV, bewildered by the sudden turn of events. I sat there, my mind spinning with confusion. What on earth had just happened? And how in the world did Sarah have any inkling about it?

I was going to go to talk with Sarah about this, but when I neared her cabin, I could hear shouting coming from James and Tammy's cabin. I couldn't understand what they were saying, but the angriness of James's voice was unmistakable.

Standing on the porch of Sarah's cabin, my hand raised to knock, a sharp cracking sound pierced the night, followed by the unmistakable sound of shattering glass coming from James and Tammy's cabin. My arm was still suspended in the air and my heart raced as I froze, listening to the unsettling sound of my property being damaged.

Sarah audibly gasped when she swung the door open. She took a few startled steps backward, losing her balance and falling to the floor.

Without hesitation, I rushed to her side, concern etched in my mind, as she groaned in pain. "Are you all right? I'm so sorry. I didn't mean to scare you."

Lying on the floor, still favoring her injured ankle, she gingerly rolled onto her side. I knelt beside her, one hand resting gently on her shoulder, the other steadying myself as the cacophony of breaking glass and escalating shouts grew louder in the background.

"What on earth is happening over there?" Sarah groaned, her voice filled with pain and irritation.

"How did you know?" I questioned.

"Know what?" she asked, her annoyance evident.

"How did you know about Tammy? That she shouldn't be trusted." I was astonished she knew that.

Sarah admitted, "I really didn't know, but she just looks like the Tammy who stole my ex. She had the same bleach-blond hair color, the same basic figure, and even the same face shape," Sarah explained with a sense of frustration. "But worst of all, she had the same fake and irritating voice.

"As soon as I saw her and heard her voice, I thought it was the Tammy I knew, and I instantly disliked her," Sarah admitted, her frustration growing. "I wanted nothing to do with her. But you might want to go over there and stop them from creating a worse disaster. Maybe call the cops?"

I sighed deeply, my brows furrowing with indecision. "If my brother wasn't involved, I'd call the authorities in a heartbeat," I admitted. "I'm not sure if it would be safe for anybody to go over there and try to stop them, but I guess I'm going to have to go anyway."

Sarah nodded in understanding as my feeling of unease intensified. The fight was escalating further, and I didn't want my brother in harm's way any longer.

"I'll go with you," she offered, her voice determined. "We can check on your brother together, and if things get out of hand, we'll call for help."

I met Sarah's eyes, her determination shining through despite the pain in her injured ankle. With a nod, I supported her as we made our way toward the commotion, worry, and apprehension in my heart.

We were almost on the porch when the door opened, and James ran out. A shiny box-like object sailed out behind him, which turned out to be the toaster, hitting him in the back. James winced and he began shouting.

"You fucking crazy bitch! You're going to pay to replace and repair everything you've destroyed!" The words shot out of his mouth like a spitting cobra's venom as he continued to yell at her.

I grabbed my phone and called 911.

By the time one of the County sheriffs arrived, it was an even more chaotic situation. Almost all of the appliances were now scattered on the ground. Chairs from the breakfast table and couch cushions were now lying in the dirt. My heart sank as I took in the extent of the damage done to my property, a sense of helplessness washing over me. This situation had spiraled far beyond control.

I stood there in stunned disbelief, my eyes fixed on the surreal sight I witnessed happening. The mini fridge now lay on the ground outside as well, the door open and all the contents scattered from where it was pushed off the porch and down the steps.

My gaze shifted to the coffee maker, which had been thrown onto the hood of James's car, with the glass carafe soon following. It left a large dent and glass covered the area. A frying pan had cracked the windshield of his car, adding further damage to an already chaotic scene.

Tammy had thrown handfuls of cutlery at James and they were scattered over the ground. Pillows lay strewn like casualties of a bizarre battle. Also among the debris were James's belongings, hatefully thrown out, adding an extra layer of madness to the scene. It was an unreal sight, one that left me struggling to comprehend how it had all come to this.

As the officer closed in on Tammy, her behavior took an even more alarming turn. She began hurling what little was left inside the cabin at him, a frenzy of desperation and defiance in her actions. When the officer attempted to restrain and cuff her, she fought back with the ferocity of a wildcat, resisting his efforts with the strength of someone twice her size.

By the time the officer finally managed to cuff her, the struggle had taken a toll on his appearance. His shirt hung torn and disheveled, having come untucked from his pants in the hectic scuffle. I could hear him reading Tammy her rights as he forcefully placed her in the back seat of his SUV.

James had taken cover behind his car and waited until it was safe to come out. He walked over to me with the most pitiful expression. "Bro, I'm so sorry about this. I had no idea she was crazy like this. Believe it or not, she comes from money and her parents are all about appearance. I'm sure that they'll pay to fix everything quickly to save themselves from a scandal. And if they don't, you can take Tammy to court and sue the crap out of her."

"Yeah." Something like this had never happened here before and I was at a loss.

As a crowd gathered, James, Sarah, and I stood amid the wreckage, contemplating our next steps. The cabin and its surroundings were a huge mess, and a far cry from the peaceful haven it had been just hours ago.

I looked at Sarah, who, despite her injured ankle, suggested, "Before we start cleaning up, we should take plenty of pictures for insurance purposes. You can deal with the legal stuff later, once you've got everything documented."

"You're going to help clean?" James asked incredulously.

"Sure. Why not?"

"Thanks, but I don't want you to get hurt any more than you've already gotten," I told her.

With remorse still evident in his eyes, James nodded in agreement. "Sarah's idea is still a good one. Let's make sure we have all the evidence we need to get this sorted out."

Amid the dark of night, we all pulled out our phones and began taking pictures of the destruction from every angle. Broken appliances, shattered glass, and scattered belongings were all meticulously documented. The flashes from our phones went off like small bursts of lightning, each click of the camera capturing the devastation and illuminating the chaos that had overtaken the once-clean grounds. It was a disheartening process, but a necessary one.

As I stepped into the cabin, a sinking feeling settled in my chest. The interior, though mostly empty, looked far worse than I had imagined. It was as if the chaos had seeped into every corner, leaving its mark on the walls, the floor, and the very air we breathed. A sense of despair filled me as I raised my phone to take pictures of the disarray.

With each picture taken, the harsh reality of the damage became more apparent. It was a daunting task, capturing the destruction, and my heart weighed heavy with the knowledge that the road ahead would be a long one to restore this space to its former tranquility.

# Chapter Six

Sarah

After we'd taken all the pictures we were going to take, we went back to my cabin, so I could ice my ankle some more. I offered to transfer all the pictures from the camera onto a flash drive. I told Hudson, I was planning on getting a pair of hiking boots tomorrow and I could get a flash drive then if he didn't already have one.

Both Hudson and James looked wrecked, as if they lost the family puppy. James looked even worse than Hudson, knowing it was because of him that Tammy had been here in the first place. It was decided that the clean-up would be better done during the day simply because of all the broken glass littering the area.

"God! I can't believe that happened. I feel so—"

Hudson cut James off. "Stop it. There's no way you could have known she was that unhinged. Don't beat yourself up. I have insurance, and you said her parents have money. It'll be all right. It'll just take time. By the way, how's your back?"

"My back? What do you mean?" James looked confused.

"She nailed you with the toaster, remember?"

James chuckled. "Oh yeah, I forgot about that. I guess it's okay."

"Yeah, well, let me see if she did any damage."

He pulled up the back of James's shirt, revealing an angry red mark that was gradually morphing into a nasty bruise. I stood up, took one of the ice packs out of the little freezer, and handed it to Hudson. I gave him a warm smile, but his sad smile broke my heart.

I wanted to wrap him in a comforting hug and take all his pain away, but James cleared his throat, breaking the moment.

"Well? How does it look?" James said impatiently, redirecting our attention back to his injury.

"If it doesn't hurt now, it probably will later," I said in the most caring voice I could muster, though that wasn't my strong suit at the moment. I continued, "You've got a pretty good-sized bruise forming there."

"Bro, can I sleep on your couch tonight?" James asked in the most miserable tone I'd heard all night.

"Of course, you know where it is when you're ready, you can also pull out the other bed. Just make sure to put a towel between you and the ice pack and whatever you plan to sleep on. And don't worry about it too much. We'll get this taken care of. Good as new."

"I'm going to go now. Sarah sorry you had to witness this, but it really was nice to meet you."

His voice carried such a profound sorrow that it tugged at my heartstrings. It was evident to me that there was more to his grief than just the events of tonight.

I gently laid my hand on Hudson's arm, preventing him from immediately following James as he moved slowly toward the RV.

Hudson covered my hand with his and looked at me questioningly.

"I think you need to find out what else is going on with James. His level of sadness was caused by more than tonight," I said with as much delicacy as possible.

He furrowed his brows. "What do you mean? What do you know? Or think you know."

I hesitated; my gaze fixed on the floor as I struggled to find the right words. "I don't know. It's just a feeling," I replied, avoiding his gaze.

I'm sure he was expecting me to say more, but there wasn't anything else I could say. 'Oh hey! By the way, sometimes I get these feelings and as long as it doesn't have anything to do with me, I'm usually right.' Yeah, I don't think so.

Hudson gently lifted my chin with his fingers and placed a soft kiss on my lips.

"Goodnight, Sarah. I'll see you in the morning," he whispered, giving me one more lingering kiss before he left.

· ♥ · ♥ · ♥ · ♥ · ♥ ·

The morning sun, with its warm and inviting light, greeted me as I made my way to my SUV. In the daylight, the extent of the mess was even more shocking than it had been with just the camera flashes at night. It resembled a small, abandoned town, after the residents had hastily left, fleeing from some impending disaster.

I stood outside the cabin, taking in a deep, rejuvenating breath. The crisp scent of the towering pines surrounded me, their earthy fragrance filling my senses and instantly bringing a sense of calm. It was as if the very essence of the Black Hills had the power to wash away worries, even in the midst of the chaos that had unfolded the night before.

I headed into Custer, determined to get the hiking boots and a flash drive to consolidate the pictures of the cabin's wreckage. It was a quick drive, and I soon found myself in a small outdoor gear store. Trying on the hiking boots was a bit of a struggle due to my still-tender ankle. The swelling had gone down significantly, but it let me know it wasn't fully healed. Nevertheless, I pressed on, knowing I needed the right gear if I was going to do anything fun during what was left of my remaining vacation.

After purchasing the items, I drove back to the RV park. When I arrived, I found Hudson and James hard at work, cleaning up the mess. I dropped off my purchases in the cabin and tied my long hair up in a ponytail.

When I started to help clean, both men looked at me with appreciation and before too long, we managed to restore some semblance of order. Only the shattered windows remained as tangible proof of what happened last night.

We made our way to Hudson's RV, where I transferred all the pictures of the frenzied aftermath onto the flash drive. As I sorted through the images and assessed the extent of the damage, my heart sank. The cost of cleaning up and replacing damaged appliances and windows, and repairing walls, not to mention repairing James's car, would be substantial.

James approached me tentatively as if he was wary about something. "Hudson told me that you thought there was... more going on besides me just being upset that Tammy did what she did. How did you know something else was wrong?" James finally asked, his voice marked with uncertainty.

I hesitated for a moment, knowing that what I was about to say would likely hurt him. "I just had a feeling, James," I replied gently. "You know. Sometimes you just know something's not right."

James let out a heavy sigh and then, as if confiding in me were a relief, he continued, "Tammy told me she's pregnant. That's why we came here, to celebrate. I was planning to propose, but after all of this, it's out of the question. But I'm going to be stuck with her in my life forever."

I knew there was more to the story, and I wanted to tread carefully. "James, it's important to be sure. Have you considered a pre-natal DNA paternity test? It's better to know now rather than later."

James looked conflicted, his brow furrowing as he considered my suggestion. "Are you saying that the baby might not be mine?"

I didn't want to spell it out directly, but I couldn't ignore my gut feeling. "James, you know, if you're not interested in staying with her... I mean... There are plenty of men out there paying for children who aren't theirs. I'm just... I'm just saying..." Uggh! "It's something to think about."

He nodded slowly with a thoughtful expression on his face. "You're right, I need to think about it."

After James had left the RV, I turned to Hudson, who had been discreetly listening. "James just told me about Tammy's pregnancy, but I don't think the baby is his. I think she's after his money. I think her parents want to cut her off once she gets married."

"But how do you know about Tammy and her parents... and what they're planning to do? Do you know them? And if she really is pregnant, why the heck was she drinking like a fish last night?"

I shook my head. "No, I've never met them. It's just a feeling. Sometimes, I..." I hesitated, the admission weighing heavily on me.

"Sometimes you what?"

"Sometimes I sense things, especially when it doesn't directly concern me. It's like really strong intuition, and it's usually pretty accurate." I watched him to gauge his reaction, but he looked more confused than anything else.

"It doesn't work for you? Well, that's not fair. So... no revelations about me then huh?" He winked as a warm smile covered his face.

I released a breath I didn't know I was holding and relaxed a little. I was never sure if the people I told were just being nice or actually were okay with my weirdness.

"No, like I said, it doesn't work for me."

Hudson tenderly cupped my cheek and leaned in to kiss me softly. The soft, slow kiss ignited my senses, and just as I was about to return the gesture, James abruptly swung open the door, interrupting us.

Exhaling loudly, Hudson whispered, "I guess you're right. It doesn't work for you."

My cheeks blazed with a sudden rush of heat, and I instinctively turned away from James.

"Bro!" James exclaimed. An awkward pause hung in the air. "Uh... Your, uh... insurance guy is here," he said, drawing out his words in a hesitant manner.

My body tingled with an uncomfortable combination of surprise and embarrassment. The sudden intrusion had jolted me from the moment Hudson, and I were sharing, leaving my nerves on edge. Heat rushed to my cheeks, and my heart raced, creating a fluttering sensation in my chest.

It was as if a rush of adrenaline had coursed through me, making every nerve ending come alive. My lips still tingled from Hudson's kiss, a lingering sensation that contrasted with the abrupt interruption. I felt way too flustered and self-conscious. It was as if an unexpected spotlight had been cast upon an all too private moment.

While Hudson spoke with the insurance agent, I retreated to my cabin, eager to give my aching ankle some much-needed rest. Carefully, I propped up my injured foot and placed an ice pack on it.

With my laptop in hand, I decided to embark on a search for enjoyable activities that wouldn't demand excessive walking. My fingers danced across the keyboard as I scoured the internet for ideas to make the most of my remaining time here, even with my limited mobility.

Just as I settled into a chair, my phone rang, and I glanced at the caller ID, surprised to see Tammy's name flashing on the screen. With a resigned sigh, I answered, bracing myself for the conversation ahead.

"Hello?" I greeted her, my voice steady but cautious.

Tammy's voice came through, laced with frustration and anger. "Sarah, you won't believe what I just found out. Warren has been cheating on me!"

I smiled sadly. Karma hit her hard with the ironic justice of having the same thing happen to her. Warren, the jerk who had cheated on me with her, was now repeating his pattern.

"I'm sorry to hear that, but once a cheater, always a cheater," I replied, my tone cool but not unkind. "But Tammy, you can't expect me to just forget what happened between us. You betrayed our friendship by getting involved with him in the first place. If you'll remember, he was my boyfriend at the time."

Tammy's voice grew defensive. "Come on, Sarah, that was in the past. Can't we just move past it?"

I took a deep breath, considering her words carefully. "Tammy, true friends don't sleep with each other's partners. I may have dodged a bullet by finding out what kind of person Warren is, but that doesn't change what you did. You're on your own with this one."

I ended the call, feeling both relief and sadness. There was a sense of relief in knowing that I had sidestepped any further heartache caused by Warren, but it didn't erase the pain of

Tammy's betrayal or the understanding that our once-close friendship had been forever ruined by her actions.

# Chapter Seven

### Hudson

Handing the flash drive to the insurance agent, he thanked me and left. I made my way to Sarah's cabin and knocked. "Sarah, you in there?"

"Come in," she called out. I entered to find her sitting at the table, her injured ankle propped up on a chair with an ice pack resting against it. My brows furrowed as I approached her.

"Hey there, how's the ankle holding up?" I asked, worried that her helping earlier caused this. "Is it hurting again?"

Sarah offered a reassuring smile. "No, it's fine," she replied. "Just icing it to reduce swelling as much as possible; it kind of feels warm. I think I've been walking on it too much today, but I'll manage."

"I hope you don't mind, but..." I picked her leg up, sat down, and placed her leg on my thigh.

Sarah chuckled and the smile that covered her blushing face warmed my heart.

"How'd it go with the insurance guy?"

"I showed him the pictures on my phone, told him about the police report, and gave him the flash drive. He said they'd look over everything and get me a check for the repairs as soon as possible. He said there shouldn't be any problems considering everything that happened. I'm just glad I called the police. He said that would help my claim."

Sarah's face brightened at the news. "That's great to hear! You'll have the cabin back in shape before you know it."

"I hope so. I'd really like the repairs to be done before winter sets in. That way, when spring arrives, it'll be ready to go."

"Not to change the subject, but I've been looking for things to do that won't put too much strain on my ankle. Got any ideas? I want to not waste the rest of my vacation."

"You know," I began, "this area might not be the national park but it's still incredibly beautiful. It's got some great trails that aren't too bad. We could go hiking together. If you get tired or your ankle starts giving you problems, I'd be happy to give you a piggyback ride back. And... I'll pack a picnic lunch for us." I hoped she'd agree to that. I wanted to feel her pressed against me again. To have her arms around me again and just be near her.

A blush crept onto her cheeks as she smiled and nodded. "That sounds wonderful, actually. I'd love to explore the area with you."

"Just let me know when you're ready to go."

"I'm ready to go now."

"I'm going to go pack us a lunch. I'll be back ASAP, and then we can hit the trail."

Sarah gave me an enthusiastic nod. "Sounds great. I'll be ready when you return."

I left her cabin and headed back to my RV to prepare our lunch. I made some barbeque sandwiches and grabbed chips, snacks, and bottled water, making sure we had enough to keep us fueled during our hike.

With lunch ready to go, I headed back to Sarah's cabin. She greeted me with a smile, and we set off toward the trailhead behind my motor home.

As we started our hike through the picturesque landscape near the Black Hills, I could see just how much she seemed to be in her element and how much she effortlessly fit in with the outdoor setting. It was as if she were born to be among nature.

She wore her new hiking boots. Their sturdy soles were much more suited for the terrain ahead than sneakers. Her blue jeans and blue T-shirt hugged her toned form. If only her jacket hadn't been tied around her waist. With her hair tied into a ponytail, she had an air of adventure about her.

We followed the winding trail, surrounded by tall trees and the soothing sounds of nature. The sun dappled through the leaves, casting a warm glow on her as we ventured deeper into the beauty of the wilderness.

As we continued along the trail, Sarah's pace slowed, and her gait became somewhat awkward. She was clearly trying to minimize any movement of her ankle. After a while, it was all too apparent that she was having a difficult time walking.

Without hesitation, I gently scooped her up into my arms, carrying her bridal style. As I lifted Sarah into my arms, a subtle gasp of surprise escaped her lips, like a soft "Oh!" accompanied by her beautiful eyes widening and a quick inhale.

I relished the sensation of cradling her close to my chest. Her floral fragrance wafted gently to meet my senses as I inhaled deeply, and her delicate scent enveloped me.

Humor sparkled in her eyes as she quipped, "Well, I guess I missed out on my piggyback ride, but this might just be better," she remarked, a playful smile gracing her lips.

The trail ended at a picturesque clearing, nestled between tall trees with sunlight filtering through their leaves. The ground was blanketed by a lush carpet of soft grass, and at the center, a flat, moss-covered rock, rose about two feet from the ground. It was ideal for our picnic. I sat Sarah down gently and began working on setting up our picnic.

"Thanks for that," she said, her voice carrying a hint of shyness. "I wish I'd brought an ice pack with me. I really didn't think it would start bothering me so soon. Sorry for all the extra work you had to do."

"I guess I'll just have to carry you back." I grinned at the thought. "Don't worry about it. You don't weigh near enough for it to be difficult for me. Besides, I kind of like carrying you like that."

A faint blush colored Sarah's cheeks, and she looked away. "So... tell me more about yourself. Any more brothers or sisters?"

"Another brother and a sister. My sister's married. I'm the oldest. What about you?"

"Two brothers, both married. I'm the youngest."

We shared stories about our families, and I was surprised to learn that her parents lived in South Dakota. She told me a bit more about her ex, I couldn't fathom how any man would betray her trust. It was a really good thing he and her ex-friend were so far away in Texas.

"Now that I've stepped away from it, I can't believe I was even attracted to him in the first place," she reflected. "I saw all the warning signs and chose to look past them. I was so stupid when it came to Warren."

"Don't beat yourself up over it. Some people just aren't very nice people. Nothing anyone can do about it."

Once we finished eating, I stowed all the containers back in the backpack and sat down beside her. "If I didn't like sleeping in a bed so much, with air conditioning or heating, I'd stay out here all the time."

She chuckled in agreement. "I know what you mean. I need those things too and a shower. Gotta have a shower," she joked.

"Agreed," I said, playfully nudging her shoulder with mine. "Let me know when you're ready to go back."

As we lounged on the rock, the conversation flowed effortlessly between us. We talked about our favorite outdoor activities, shared funny childhood stories, and discussed our bucket lists. The more we talked, the more I found myself drawn to Sarah's warmth and the effortless way she made me feel at ease.

"Thank you for bringing me here. This place is amazing, so beautiful and peaceful," she said, her shyness resurfacing. It was as if she couldn't quite believe she deserved to be appreciated.

"Once you move up here permanently, I'll be happy to take you wherever you want to go. It's more fun when someone goes with you. I don't really go to many places by myself. It's kind of lonely, so I'm glad you're here."

Sarah gazed at me. "It sounds like a good idea. I'd like that."

Putting my hand on the back of her neck, I drew her to me. I placed a soft kiss on her lips, but soon the kisses became more needy. Our tongues danced around each other, and I could feel myself heating up to a dangerous level. I wanted her.

Laying her back, I ran my hand down her side and rested it on the top of her jeans. One of her hands roamed my chest and the other one found its way under my shirt. When her delicate hand touched bare skin, I knew if it continued, I'd want all of her, not just the kisses and not just the touching.

I was about to unbutton and unzip her pants when the sound of a nearby tree branch snapped, making us both jump. I began scanning the area for predators.

"Uh… sorry bro. Didn't mean to startle you." At least James had the decency to look a little uncomfortable.

Sarah giggled, her cheeks flushed with embarrassment as she turned away from him.

I let out an exasperated groan as James stopped us once again. His timing couldn't have been worse, not once, but twice now! He and I were going to have to have a little talk.

"Sorry to interrupt, but Angie is looking for you." James shuffled the dirt around his foot while he spoke. "I'll just uh… be leaving now."

"Wait! You can carry the backpack." I told him and then grinned at Sarah. "Looks like you'll get your piggyback ride after all!"

She turned a bright shade of pink, but her smile was beautiful.

Sarah climbed on my back, and we started the trek back to the campground. With her legs locked around my hips, her arms around my shoulders and chest, and her breasts pressed against my back, I was enjoying myself. She rested her chin on my arm and spoke in hushed tones.

Her warm breath brushed against my neck as she spoke, sharing stories about another one of her favorite hiking spots and the places she'd like to see. We discussed everything from our favorite books to our dreams of traveling to distant places, but we avoided talking about what just happened.

I dropped Sarah off at her cabin and went to the campground office, not expecting any major surprises. Angie glanced up from the computer, her expression hesitant. "Hudson," she began, "I hate to be the bearer of bad news, but we received a reservation for a cabin from Virginia last night after we closed. She's scheduled to arrive in two days."

My stomach churned at the mention of Virginia's name. Our breakup had been far from amicable. Her possessiveness, jealousy, entitlement, and greed had been the reason for our split. The memories of our arguments and the toxic dynamic between us resurfaced, casting a shadow over what had otherwise been a nearly perfect day.

Virginia always had a double standard when it came to relationships. It was perfectly acceptable for her to have guy friends and spend time with them whenever she pleased. But if she ever caught me even glancing in the direction of another woman, all hell would break loose. During what I thought was our final conversation, I had made it clear that I wanted nothing more to do with her.

Yet, it seemed like Virginia hadn't taken my words seriously. She had this self-centered way of viewing the world where all her actions were justified, and anything that didn't align with her narrative was simply glossed over. It was just too frustrating to deal with her.

Leaving the office, I knew I had to have a conversation with Sarah about this unexpected turn of events. Virginia's arrival had the potential to create unnecessary tension, and I wanted to make sure Sarah was prepared for the situation. It wasn't a conversation I was looking forward to, but it was necessary to ensure that Sarah's stay wouldn't be overshadowed by the drama Virginia was sure to bring with her.

# Chapter Eight

Hudson

I saw Sarah through the window of her cabin working on her laptop, her leg on a chair, and an ice pack on her ankle. I wasn't looking forward to this conversation, but I also knew it was important for her to know this in advance. Taking a deep breath, I knocked.

"Come in."

"Sarah." I stood, trying to keep my tone steady, "there's something I need to tell you. Angie just told me that Virginia, my ex-girlfriend, has reserved a cabin here and is arriving in two days."

Sarah looked up from her laptop, her expression curious but guarded. "Okay?" she said drawing out the word.

I hesitated for a moment, choosing my words carefully. "Well… our breakup wasn't exactly friendly, and she's… an extremely self-centered person. If she's coming to try to get back with me, and I swear I'm not interested in her in the slightest, she'll… she'll try something, and no one can stop her. I need you to know this because, and I'm not joking, she's extremely possessive and jealous and she won't take it well if she sees me even talking to you. And I definitely want to… talk to you." I wanted to add 'among other things,' but I stopped myself.

Sarah nodded, her eyes growing wary. "I see. I'm, uh... is she a... violent person? I mean, do you think you'll have to worry about another cabin getting destroyed?"

I sighed and considered how to describe Virginia without holding back. "Honestly, I wouldn't put it past her, but I hope not. She's the kind of person who's micro-managing, narcissistic, lying, manipulative, and a bully."

"So... a pillar of society then." She looked at her laptop and closed the lid. "Hudson, I don't want to cause you any more problems than you've already dealt with. If it'll make things easier for you, I can check out a few days early and—"

"No!" I practically shouted. "I don't want you to leave early. I want you to stay. I've enjoyed the past few days more than all the days in the past year combined. It's going to be hard enough when you have to go back to Texas next week. I already know I'm going to miss you. I want you to stay."

"You're going to miss me?" she asked in a surprised tone. "I... I'm going to miss you too," she said quietly.

I knelt beside her chair, and with a tender touch, I cradled her face in my hands before our lips met. Her soft, inviting mouth drew me in like a magnetic force, and when our tongues met, it was as if time stood still. I was falling in love with her. Her gentle nature was a soothing balm to my soul, and the mere thought of her leaving sent a sharp pain radiating from my heart, a discomfort so intense it was almost unbearable.

"Wow..." Sarah said as if in a daze. "That was... wow."

Sarah and I shared another lingering kiss, our emotions whirling in the air around us. When we finally parted, our breaths were ragged, and the connection between us felt stronger than ever. I could see the same longing in her eyes that mirrored my own feelings.

Unable to hold back any longer, I spoke softly, my voice barely above a whisper, "Sarah, I don't want you to leave. I want you to stay here with me."

She met my gaze, her eyes filled with uncertainty and vulnerability. "Hudson, I... I want to stay too, but I have responsibilities back in Texas. I don't have a choice."

I nodded, understanding the practicalities, but the thought of being without her for even a week felt unbearable. "I know, and I respect that. But can we make the most of the time we have left together?"

A hesitant smile graced her lips, and she reached out to touch my cheek. "Yes, let's make the most of it."

As I was leaning in for another kiss, someone knocked on the door loudly. I groaned in frustration. my head dropped, and I rubbed my eyelids. "If that's James, I'm going to kill him!" I muttered under my breath as I opened the door.

"Bro, she called back. She's coming tomorrow," James blurted out, a hint of urgency in his voice as he tried to catch his breath. "I figured you'd want to know ASAP!"

Exasperated, I hissed at him. "Dude, you have the worst timing."

"Oh...uh... sorry about that." Well, at least he sounded a little apologetic.

James had the audacity to disrupt the moment... again, but then, a soft, melodic giggle escaped Sarah's lips. The corners of my mouth tugged into a reluctant smile despite my irritation.

Sarah's giggle continued, filling the room with her infectious laughter. It was as if her joy had the power to chase away any lingering frustration. I couldn't help but chuckle alongside her, realizing that sometimes, life's interruptions could lead to unexpected moments of humor.

James, sensing the shift in the atmosphere, joined in the laughter, making light of his poorly timed entrance. We shared a brief exchange before he excused himself, leaving Sarah and me with the promise of privacy once more.

"Just curious, how much longer is James going to be here? If he's here long enough, his habit of interrupting you could come in handy if your ex is here with the idea of getting back with you."

It seemed the moment was lost again but Sarah could be right about James. "I don't know. He was only planning on being here for about a week, but given the Tammy situation, things might change. I'll check with him."

### Sarah

After James left, I couldn't help but think about his timing. Part of me was relieved by his interruptions, but another part of me was disappointed because I was genuinely attracted to Hudson and was curious to see where this, whatever this was, might lead.

I leaned back in my chair, my gaze fixed on the serene landscape outside the cabin window. After James's latest interruption, my mind was in a whirlwind of thoughts, and I decided it was probably a good time to tell him some of them.

"You know, Hudson," I began, my voice thoughtful, "I've been doing a lot of thinking lately. These interruptions, as inconvenient as they are, have given me some time to think."

Hudson turned his attention towards me, his warm brown eyes locking onto mine. "Think about what?"

I took a deep breath, trying to find the right words. "I've really enjoyed spending time with you, and I won't deny that I'm attracted to you, but..." I hesitated, "I have to consider my own situation. I don't even live in this area yet, and with your ex coming to the campground, things seem a bit... complicated. Couldn't you just cancel her reservation?"

He nodded, his expression understanding. "I get what you're saying. It's true; things are a bit complicated right now. And if I canceled it, she'd come anyway."

I continued, "I want to see where this could go between us, but I also don't want to make any rash decisions. I don't want to get hurt again. I need to make sure my living situation is more permanent. And... well your ex could be a real problem."

Hudson's gaze remained fixed on me; his eyes filled with a bit of sadness. "I understand. It's important for you to take things more slowly."

A sense of relief washed over me as he voiced his understanding. "Thank you. I hope you know that I genuinely enjoy your company, and I'm looking forward to spending more time with you, but..."

A gentle smile played across his lips as he replied, "I think I understand what you mean. So... I'm guessing that means the most we'll be doing is kissing." He looked at me with the most adorable, dejected face.

I couldn't help but chuckle at his cute expression, and I reached out to gently touch his hand. "Well, kissing is a pretty good start, don't you think?"

Hudson's eyes twinkled as he grinned. "It's an excellent start."

Reaching out, I placed my hand against his neck and caressed his cheek with my thumb. "Not to change the subject again, but I'm tired of sitting in the cabin. Do you want to take a little walk? Maybe on flatter ground?"

"Is your ankle any better? Do you mind if I take a look?" His hand moved to the back of my neck. "After a kiss."

His wicked grin belied the tender kiss. If I wasn't careful, I knew I might just fall head over heels for this incredible man. The thought both thrilled and terrified me.

The bruise looked much worse than it felt. When Hudson pulled my sock off, the bruise had developed into a deep, almost regal, shade of purple at its center, surrounded by a chaotic dance of dark blues and greens. It reminded me of an abstract painting... kind of.

I knew that I should stay off it, but I was on vacation, dammit! I wanted to see and experience as much of this place as I could. I wanted to go places and do things and my stupid ankle was getting in the way of nearly everything.

"It looks worse than it really is. And yes... I still want to go for a walk."

"I don't know. Maybe I should just give you a piggyback ride. The more you stay off it the better. Besides, you should probably be using crutches anyway."

"Another piggyback ride. Sounds like a plan. Okay, I'm going to tell you something I might regret saying out loud." I wished I hadn't said anything, but it was too late.

"Tell me."

"Maybe not."

"Oh no. You started it, you have to finish it."

"Fine," I said with mock exasperation. "I like being carried by you. I like... being carried by you." Why couldn't I stop myself from saying anything?

"Oh no, you don't get off that easy. What's the second like?" he said with a chuckle.

"I like the way you feel and... yeah, that's it." I didn't want to say I liked the way he smelled when I was that close to him.

"You know... if I give you a piggy-front ride..."

When he picked me up under the arms and pulled me onto his chest, I wrapped my legs around his back. He pushed me up further with his arms under my butt until we were at eye level.

The expression on his face spoke volumes. "I don't regret you saying that out loud. I like carrying you. I like the way you feel in my arms or on my back or front." His lascivious smile gave me chills. Chills that made me want more from him.

He began slowly kissing his way up my neck and finally reached my lips. What he was doing to me now, should be considered a crime. I wanted him. Resting my arms on his shoulders, I held the back of his head. His soft brown hair felt silky, and I could have stayed like this for a long time before I was ready to move.

We kissed. A passionate kiss like none before. Our tongues united in a sexy dance meant only for us. As I shifted to get closer, I could feel myself heating up to a dangerous level. But we were already as close as we could get, and it still wasn't enough.

I couldn't stop the moan of pleasure I was feeling. I was about to give in to my desires when a loud, almost desperate knocking came from the door again.

"Bro! She's here!"

Anger flashed in his eyes, but then it disappeared. "I think I was beginning to get a little too hot," he said apologetically.

"Yeah, me too," I confessed.

The smile on his face conveyed his thoughts perfectly and I was certain they matched mine.

# Chapter Nine

### Sarah

Hudson left my cabin, and I watched as his expression shifted from irritation to caution when he saw Victoria come out of the campground office. She was a striking woman, tall, elegant, polished, and had confidence that oozed from her every move. Her presence seemed to fill the space around her, making it hard for anyone to ignore her.

Hudson approached her with a cautious nod, his posture tense. They exchanged a few words, but I couldn't hear the conversation. The air between them crackled with tension, and it was clear that their history was anything but amicable.

I couldn't help but feel a pang of curiosity mixed with a touch of jealousy. Hudson had been nothing but kind and respectful to me since we'd met, but the thought of him having a history with someone as striking as Victoria left a knot in my stomach.

I tried to distract myself by tidying up my cabin, but my thoughts kept drifting back to their meeting. Whatever they were discussing, it was clear that it had the potential to disrupt the peace we'd found in our time together at the campground.

My heart pounded in my chest as I watched the tension in Hudson's jaw and the sharpness in his eyes when he spoke to Victoria. There was no mistaking the anger simmering just beneath the surface. As I moved out to the porch and sat down, Victoria turned her gaze toward me. Our eyes locked, and I felt a rush of emotions — unease, curiosity, a twinge of apprehension, a touch of intrigue, and still, the jealousy was there.

Victoria began walking toward me, her animated conversation with Hudson continuing. She was being a bit too clingy for my taste. "...coming out of her cabin. Why were you in there, baby?"

"Stop calling me baby!" Hudson spat as he quickened his pace to catch up with her.

Victoria stopped in front of me and looked at Hudson with one eyebrow raised and then at me.

"This is Sarah, she's a guest here," Hudson "introduced" me.

Victoria stepped closer to me, a deceitfully sweet smile on her mouth, her eyes flickering with something more ominous. "Sarah, dear, I've heard so much about you," she cooed, her words dripping with insincerity.

I met her gaze; my expression was calm and unreadable. "Oh, have you? That's excessively difficult to believe."

Ignoring my reply, she continued in an arrogant tone, "Hudson and I go way back. We have quite the history together."

I didn't flinch, maintaining my composure. "Yes, I'm sure you do. It must be nice to catch up with old friends."

Her smile tightened, and she leaned in closer, lowering her voice. "Just remember, dear, Hudson and I have a special relationship. It's something that can't be easily replicated."

I held her gaze, refusing to back down. "Relationships are important, aren't they? But sometimes, it's the new ones that matter most. And honestly, I wouldn't want to replicate your relationship with Hudson. From what I've heard... it didn't end well... for you."

Hudson started to step in, but I subtly shook my head and he stopped. It was clear that Victoria was doing her best to send a message to me to back off, but I had no intention of letting her intimidation tactics influence me.

Victoria's smile wavered, and she hesitated, taking a step backward. Her eyes narrowed as she cast glances between Hudson and me. Without a doubt, she saw me as her competition, someone to be beaten and she did **not** like me.

Hudson sighed as she turned and walked away. "Sarah, I'm sorry about that."

I grinned. "Don't worry about it. She's not the first narcissist I've dealt with. She's not even the worst. She **is** quite sure of herself though, isn't she?"

Hudson laughed awkwardly and apologized again. "I just want you to be careful. There's no telling what she'll do if she thinks you're standing in the way of what she wants."

"Yeah, people like her tend to react... strongly when they don't get their way." A thought crossed my mind. "Did James tell you how long he's staying?"

Hudson grinned. "Worried about James interrupting us again?"

I couldn't help but smile. "No, I was just thinking that you might need backup."

"Is this one of the feelings you get?" He raised an eyebrow and looked concerned.

"It could be. I don't know." When it came to Hudson, things were rapidly dimming in that regard. I didn't know if it meant his life was intertwined with mine enough that I wouldn't get things for him or if I was worried about Victoria worming her way back into Hudson's life and me getting hurt again.

"I'll have to ask him. With everything that's happened lately, I forgot to ask. Victoria was only supposed to be here for a week starting in two days but with her, there's no telling." Hudson looked almost defeated. This unexpected wrench in the works was clearly something he wasn't prepared for.

"Why don't you talk to him and find out?" I gently suggested.

I sat in the cabin, mulling over the recent events, when I heard approaching footsteps. Dread washed over me as I realized who it was — Victoria. She barged into the cabin without knocking, her demeanor completely different from before.

Her voice dripped with malice as she began her attack. "You know, Sarah," she sneered, "I've heard a lot about you. Hudson doesn't usually bring guests here, but I suppose he felt sorry for you."

I clenched my fists, struggling to maintain my composure. Before I could respond, she continued, "You should know your place. Hudson and I have a history. You're just a temporary distraction for him until I'm back in his life for good."

I took a deep breath, my patience was wearing thin, but I forced myself to stay calm. I knew she was trying to provoke a reaction from me, but I was determined not to give her the satisfaction. "Victoria, I'm not here to interfere with anyone's past. Hudson and I are just getting to know each other. Maybe it's time for you to move on."

She scoffed, leaning closer. "You think you can replace me? You're nothing, just a passing fling!"

Victoria's sharp words continued to cut through the air like a dagger. She clearly wasn't satisfied with my lack of reaction and pressed on relentlessly.

"You really think Hudson would choose you over me?" she taunted. "Look at you. You're plain, poorly dressed, and you're not even pretty. Look at me, I'm gorgeous. No man alive can resist me. If I want them, I get them. And you have no fashion sense whatsoever. He's no fool. He knows you're not worth his time. He's just playing with you. He's just trying to make me jealous. I can tell he wants me back and nothing you do… **nothing** you do will change that!"

I gritted my teeth, determined not to let her get under my skin. "Victoria, I'm not trying to replace anyone. Hudson and I are simply enjoying each other's company."

Her laughter was cold and mocking. "Enjoying each other's company? Is that what he's told you? You're so naive."

She spoke with such conviction that it was difficult to remember that this is what a narcissist does. I felt my anger simmering beneath the surface but forced myself to stay composed. "I don't need your approval or your opinion of me. My relationship with Hudson is none of your concern."

She leaned in closer, her eyes burning with rage. "You're in way over your head, Sarah. You don't know what you're dealing with. I can make things very difficult for you."

I met her gaze with a steely resolve. "Threats won't work on me, Victoria. If you have an issue with Hudson, you need to talk to him about it. I'm not getting involved in your drama."

Victoria's expression shifted from anger to frustration as she realized her attempts to manipulate me were failing. Before she could retort, Hudson returned, effectively ending the confrontation. But the venomous words she had spewed lingered in the air, leaving me fuming and determined to stand my ground against this unwelcome rival.

Before I could retort, Hudson burst back into the cabin. He didn't waste any time, warning Victoria sternly, "Victoria! I could hear you all the way outside. If you don't stop this right now, I'll throw you out of the campground."

Victoria's demeanor shifted instantly, but she shot me one last venomous glance before storming out. Hudson watched her go, his expression tense, before turning to me with a reassuring smile. "I'm sorry you had to deal with that. She won't bother you anymore."

I sighed in relief, grateful for Hudson's support. "Thanks, Hudson. I really hope so, but I'm not holding my breath."

Hudson opened his mouth to say something, but a soft tapping on the door stopped him. He jerked the door open, and James took a few steps back.

"Bro, what the hell? James said startled.

Hudson's shoulders slumped and he visibly relaxed. "Victoria was just here. I thought she was coming back. Sorry. Come in."

James's smirk was a welcome sight as he walked into the cabin. His playful tone provided some relief from the tension I had just experienced with Victoria.

"Oh yeah? What did the wicked witch of the galaxy want?" he teased, taking a seat at the table. "I'm sure it's nothing good. I'm so glad you dumped her sorry butt. What'd she do this time?"

I let out a sigh of relief, grateful for James' interruption this time. His easygoing demeanor was a stark contrast to Victoria's poisonous actions.

"Victoria just wanted to... catch up," I replied, choosing my words carefully to avoid revealing the full extent of our encounter. "You know how it is."

James raised an eyebrow, clearly sensing there was more to the story but deciding not to press further. "Bro, you're so much better off without her, that's for sure."

"James, how much longer are you planning on staying?" Hudson inquired, a hint of concern in his voice.

James chuckled playfully. "Why? Trying to get rid of me, huh?"

Hudson responded with a raised eyebrow, not uttering a word.

"I was planning on leaving on Sunday. Why?" James inquired.

Hudson hesitated for a moment before speaking, his voice filled with a bit of seriousness and a hint of humor. "Think you could stay for another week? Or at least until Victoria leaves."

James quirked an eyebrow and leaned back in his chair. "Why? You think the witch will cast a spell on you or worse... curse you?" With a goofy grin, he waggled his eyebrows.

Hudson grinned back, appreciating James' sense of humor. "I just thought I might need some backup."

"It shouldn't be a problem. Let me just call the parents and let them know I won't be coming in to work next week," James said as he dialed the number. He placed his phone on the table, turning on the speaker function.

"James! You're supposed to be on vacation. What's wrong?" The woman's voice had a strange mix of excitement and worry, carrying through the speaker with a touch of warmth.

"Hi, Mom," James replied, his tone reassuring. "Nothing's wrong. Or at least nothing right now. Hudson's here."

"Hudson, sweetheart, we miss you. You need to come and visit sometime soon," his mom chimed, her voice tinged with sadness.

"Mom, you know I have a business to run here. Maybe sometime when the business closes down for the winter."

"Oh, I can't wait! I miss you." his mom exclaimed eagerly. "Honey, Hudson's on the phone."

"Hudson, my boy. When are you coming to visit? We miss you, son," His dad added warmly.

"Hi, Dad. I miss you too," Hudson replied, his voice filled with affection. "I'll figure something out to come see you. Or you two could come here too, you know."

As the conversation continued between Hudson, James, and their parents, I couldn't help but feel a twinge of homesickness for my own family. The warmth and familiarity of their interactions made me miss my parents even more.

Hudson and James shared stories and laughter with their folks, not really discussing much of anything, just enjoying the conversation. It was heartwarming to witness their love for their family, but it also highlighted the miles that usually separated me from mine.

As the two men ended the call, a bittersweet feeling washed over me, and I craved the comforting presence of my parents even more. It was moments like these that made me realize how much I missed them and how glad I was that I'd be living so much closer to them soon.

# Chapter Ten

### Hudson

As James and I continued speaking with our parents, I noticed a subtle change in Sarah's demeanor. Her once-bright expression had faded, replaced by a hint of sorrow. It tugged at my heart, and I decided to address the growing sadness in Sarah, ending the call with my parents. I leaned closer to her and whispered, "Hey, are you okay?" She looked up at me, her eyes reflecting sorrow.

"I'm fine," she replied softly, though her eyes told a different story.

"Sarah." I gently chided her. "I can see it in your eyes. Something's wrong."

"I just miss my parents. The last time I saw them was Christmas. And now, they're on an overseas vacation and won't be back for another two weeks. Once they get back, I'm planning to visit them, but... well, I just miss them."

I nodded understandingly, realizing that Sarah was in a bit of a tough spot. "I'll see what I can do to take your mind off it, at least for a while anyway. We'll make the most of your remaining time here, and once you move here, you can go see them more often."

Just as we were settling back into our conversation, James excused himself from the cabin. He promised not to interrupt us any further, but I exchanged a knowing look with Sarah. Deep down, we both suspected that James might not be able to resist the urge to interrupt us again.

Sarah and I spent the next couple of days getting to know each other better. We went on short walks around the campground, enjoying the natural beauty of the Black Hills area. I was careful to choose trails that wouldn't put too much strain on Sarah's ankle, and I even carried a picnic basket to surprise her with a relaxing lunch in a peaceful spot.

As the week drew to a close, we laughed and shared quiet moments together. I was drawn to Sarah's warmth and gentle nature. We discovered shared interests, talked about our families, and even discussed our plans for when she returned. And more importantly, both James and Victoria stayed away.

Saturday arrived all too soon, and it was time for Sarah to leave. I could see the sadness in her eyes as she packed her belongings. I knew her leaving was inevitable, but I felt a profound sense of loss, no matter how short it would be. We'd shared a special week together, and I didn't want it to end.

We stood outside her cabin, the autumn leaves falling around us, creating a picturesque backdrop. Sarah hugged me tightly, tears glistening in her eyes. "Thank you for everything, Hudson. You made my time here unforgettable."

I held her close, my own emotions threatened to surface. "I know it's only a week, but I'm going to miss you, Sarah. Promise me you'll call when you get home. I want to make sure you're okay."

Sarah nodded, her voice barely above a whisper. "I will. I promise."

With a final, lingering kiss, we reluctantly let go of each other. I watched as Sarah got into her SUV and drove away. I couldn't wait for the day when Sarah would return to my life once more.

Victoria must have been watching because as soon as Sarah was gone, she left her cabin and headed toward me. I braced myself for an irritating encounter as she approached, wearing a calculating smile.

"Hudson, baby, it's been too long," she purred, trying to lean in for a kiss. I sidestepped her advances, irritated with everything about her.

"Victoria, we've been over this. It's not going to happen. We're done and I don't want anything to do with you, and for God's sake, stop calling me baby!" I replied firmly.

Undeterred, she continued to flirt and sweet-talk me, attempting to reignite a spark that had long since been drowned by the ocean of regret I had from ever knowing her. Sarah was coming back. I wasn't about to take the chance of her finding out that I did something so stupid as to be with Victoria.

Just as Victoria was about to make another attempt, James showed up, coming to my rescue. He greeted us with a wide grin, disrupting the tense atmosphere.

"Hey, bro, what's going on?" James asked, feigning obliviousness to the underlying tension, though he was well aware of Victoria's history with me.

Victoria quickly realized that her advances were falling flat. She excused herself with an exaggerated sigh and a toss of her hair, sauntering off with one last sultry glance back at me. Her voice dripped with honey as she promised to return later, leaving the lingering stench of her overpowering perfume in the air, like the sickly-sweet smell of someone ill.

Night fell, and I retired to my RV. However, as I settled in, I heard a fumbling at the door. It was Victoria, attempting to sneak in. Fortunately, I'd locked the door, and she couldn't just barge in like she did with Sarah.

"Victoria! What do you want?" I asked harshly through the door.

She began to plead with me, her voice laced with desperation. "Hudson, baby, please, just let me in. I miss you so much. I can't stand being away from you. I know you miss me."

I wanted her gone. If I'd seen the online booking, I would have tried to cancel it immediately, but I knew it wouldn't do any good. It was clear that she wasn't ready to accept the reality that I wasn't interested in her anymore.

After a prolonged silence, Victoria finally relented. "Fine, I'll go for now, but I'll be back tomorrow morning. We need to talk."

Once she left, I felt like I could breathe again, and I sagged onto the couch. I heard muffled laughter coming from the other bedroom where James had been listening to the entire exchange. I had to chuckle at the absurdity of the situation.

# AUTUMN WHISPERS

I opened the door to James's room, and he greeted me with a wide grin, his laughter still evident in his eyes. "Bro, she's something else, isn't she? I mean, sneaking around in the middle of the night? Classic Victoria."

I laughed along with him. "Yeah, you could say that. I thought she might try something like this, but I didn't expect her to be so persistent."

James shook his head in amusement. "Well, that's Victoria for you. She doesn't give up easily. She really can't believe that there's anybody who wouldn't be interested in her."

We both shared a knowing look, acknowledging the unfortunate history I had with Victoria. It was clear that her return was going to complicate things further.

"So, what's the plan now?" James asked.

I sighed, not entirely sure how to proceed. "I'll deal with her tomorrow when she comes back. Right now, I need some rest. It's been a rough day."

James patted me on the back. "Sounds like a plan. Just remember, I'm here if you need any backup."

With that, we both retreated to our respective rooms. I couldn't shake off the unease that Victoria's actions had stirred within me. The unsettling encounter left me on edge, and I wondered, and dreaded, what the next day might bring.

My phone chimed. It was a message from Sarah. I'd rather hear her voice, but a smile covered my face, nonetheless.

Sarah

> Hey Hudson, I'm back home now. I'm in ranger housing right now. Don't want to disturb anyone in the house by making a call.

Hudson

> No problem. Glad u made it back ok. Text is fine. How's it going over there?

Sarah

> It's good. Sorry… but I'm worried about Victoria. She wants u back. Saw her heading 2 u when I was leaving.

I sighed. Considering what she'd been through with her ex, I understood her concerns about Victoria.

> **Hudson**
> Yeah, she's persistent. Don't worry, James is my bodyguard. Lol. If she becomes a problem, James will interrupt. Already talked to him about it.

> **Sarah**
> Thx, Appreciate that. U understand, right?

I smiled sadly at her message.

> **Hudson**
> I do. Not joking, even if u weren't in the pic, she's not worth it. Don't worry.

> **Sarah**
> Thx for understanding. Know we haven't known each other 4 long, but u mean a lot 2 me.

> **Hudson**
> Same here. Always here for u.

> **Sarah**
> Grateful 4 that. C u soon.

> **Hudson**
> Can't wait.

> **Sarah**
> Night Hudson.

> **Hudson**
> Sweet dreams.

Unfortunately, Victoria kept her promise and returned the next morning. She wasted no time in launching another attempt to sway me back into her life. But the more she tried, the angrier I became.

"I don't know how many times I have to say it, Victoria," I hissed through gritted teeth, "it's over! We're done! I don't want you anywhere near me or my life ever again!"

She pouted, trying to appear vulnerable, but her desperation was clear. "Baby, you can't just throw away everything we had. Think about all the good times."

I scoffed. "The 'good times,' Victoria? Do you mean the constant drama, jealousy, and manipulation? Yeah, those were real gems. The absolute best of the best!"

James, who had been observing the whole debacle, couldn't contain his disbelief any longer. He shook his head in astonishment from his spot in the background, clearly not believing the audacity of Victoria's persistence.

I continued, my anger simmering just below the surface, ready to explode. "I've moved on, Victoria. I have someone in my life now who actually cares about me and doesn't try to control every aspect of my life."

Victoria's face contorted in frustration, and she took a step closer, ignoring the warning in my eyes. "Hudson... baby, I love you. We can work through this. Just give us another chance."

That was the final straw. My temper flared, and I snapped, "No, Victoria! We can't. Stay until your reservation is over or don't, but know this, I really just want you to leave, and I don't want you coming back here! If you keep this up, I'll kick you out of your cabin and off my property! And... if I have to call the police, I will! Do you understand?"

Her eyes widened as the weight of my words sank in. Without another word, she pivoted on her heels and strode away. My tension began to dissipate but the anger lingered. It was like a storm had passed, leaving behind scattered debris in its wake.

A sense of triumph mingled with the remnants of anger and irritation. I couldn't deny that standing my ground with her felt good, but the encounter had also left me drained. Watching her retreating figure, I wondered if this would be the end of her persistent attempts or if she would find some other way to disrupt my life once again. The uncertainty of it all weighed on my mind, but for the moment, I relished in the quiet that had finally descended upon my campground.

James strolled up to me, a grin on his face. "Hey, bro, you all right?"

I nodded, appreciating his concern. "Yeah, I'm good. Thanks for sticking around. There's no telling what she would do if it were just the two of us."

He chuckled. "No problem, man. She's like a pit bull with a bone once she sets her sights on something."

I sighed, leaning against the side of my RV. "Tell me about it. I just hope that that was the end of it."

James raised an eyebrow. Understanding and amusement laced his voice. "You really think she's done?"

I shrugged, uncertainty gnawing at me. "Honestly, I don't know. But after what I told her last night and today, you'd think she'd get the message."

James let out a low whistle. "Bro, you've got to remember, for someone like her, the idea that there's someone who wouldn't want her is probably unthinkable. She's used to getting what she wants."

I ran a hand through my hair, frustration building. "Unfortunately, I know you're right. I just hope my message gets through her ego sooner rather than later."

He clapped me on the shoulder. "Don't worry too much, bro. I've got your back, but I don't think she's done yet. Just stay on your toes."

As James walked away, his words echoed in my mind. I wondered how much more drama Victoria would bring into my life before she finally accepted and admitted, to herself, that I was no longer interested.

# Chapter Eleven

### Hudson

Sarah and I had been texting regularly, but I really wanted to see her beautiful face. We set up a time for a video call after she was done with work. I'd already installed an app that recorded video calls so I could see her and hear her voice again. I wanted to give Sarah a virtual tour of some of the places I wanted to take her when she moved back. I initiated the call, and her smiling face appeared on my screen.

"Hey there," I greeted her with a grin.

"Hey, Hudson. How's your day going?" Sarah replied, her eyes sparkling.

I explained my plan to go on a hike and show her some scenic spots around the campground. She seemed excited about the idea, so I started the hike, holding my phone up to show her the beautiful landscape.

As we chatted and I showed her around, I felt content just getting to talk and spend time with her. It wasn't as good as her being here, but it was better than nothing. I was looking forward to the day when we could explore these places together in person.

My heart sank as I spotted Victoria approaching in the distance. She must have seen me leaving for my hike. I quickly explained to Sarah about Victoria and asked her to stay quiet. I was so happy my call with Sarah was being recorded. I held my phone near my chest.

Victoria walked up to me, and our conversation quickly turned into an argument. She tried, again, to convince me to give us another chance.

I raised my voice, my anger getting the better of me. "There isn't a single thing on Earth that would make that happen!"

Fury flashed in her eyes as she shot back, her voice seething with venom. "You're going to regret that. No one, and I mean no one, tells me no!"

Victoria stormed off, leaving me alone again. I returned to my RV, still on the call with Sarah. As we continued talking, I noticed a sheriff's SUV and two police officers get out of it and head toward Victoria's cabin.

My heartbeat sped up as I watched the officers closely. They spoke with Victoria. She appeared disheveled and seemed to have turned the waterworks on. Her clothes were torn and dirty, and her usually perfect hair was messy. My anxiety grew as I feared she might accuse me of something I would never do.

Sure enough, there was a knock on my RV door, and panic welled up inside me. I knew I needed a plan. Quickly, I explained the situation to Sarah, asking her to stay on the call.

I opened the door to find Darren, someone who I'd known since high school, and his partner standing there. "Darren, can I help you?"

Darren glanced at his partner and then asked, "May we come in?"

I chose my words carefully, aware that saying the wrong thing could make things worse for me. Now, I was certain she'd accused me of something. "I understand you're probably just doing your job, but why are you here in the first place?"

The other officer responded, "We just need to ask you some questions." His hand rested on the butt of his gun.

My heart raced as I asked, "What do you mean? Am I being accused of something?"

Darren's tone was stern as he said, "Things will be a lot easier if you just cooperate with us."

I couldn't believe this was happening. Darren knew me from way back. He should know I wouldn't do whatever Victoria claimed.

"Officer, you need to listen to me!" Sarah protested. "Hudson's been on a video call with me for about an hour now! Whatever Victoria told you is a lie. Hudson! I'll hang up and you can show them the video. Officers, please watch the video. Hudson hasn't done anything to Victoria!" Sarah's pleading voice came over the phone's speaker.

Darren smirked. "Is that your girlfriend? Relax Tony. I think we need to go inside and talk."

I reluctantly agreed to let them in. We sat at the table, and I explained the situation. James was already sitting there, and his presence seemed to add credibility to my story.

After some convincing, the two officers agreed to watch the video. I quickly told Sarah I'd call her later. She hung up, and we watched as the video clearly showed that less than an hour ago, Victoria was unharmed, and I hadn't seen her since our confrontation.

"You need to send that video to me," Darren stated with an air of authority.

"It's probably way too big to email. Give me a sec, and I'll transfer it to a flash drive. I bought one to replace the one Sarah bought for us." James offered.

I was thinking that Sarah would probably rather have the money but didn't say so. I was just happy his brain works the way it does.

James transferred the video and gave it to Darren. They thanked James and me for our help and headed back to Victoria's cabin.

I took a deep breath and called Sarah back. I gave her the details of what happened as I peered out my window, watching the cabin Victoria was in.

"They're taking her away, and yeah, she's in cuffs. They're putting her in the backseat. I guess that means they arrested her," I reported, relief flooding through me. The weight that had been pressing on my chest lifted, and I could finally breathe again. "I can't thank you enough for being on that call, Sarah. You just saved me from a nightmare."

I could hear the warmth of Sarah's smile on the phone as she replied, "Well, I'm glad you called." With a little trepidation, she added, "I just hope it's really over now, and she's gone for good."

## Sarah

After ending my phone call with Hudson, I felt a wave of relief wash over me. Our conversation reassured me and strengthened my trust in him. I savored the warmth of the closeness we were already sharing.

But just as I was reveling in the sense of security Hudson had given me, a sudden, forceful knock on my door shattered the tranquility of the moment. My heart raced as I went to answer it, only to find an unexpected and unwelcome face on the other side. It was Warren, and his expression was filled with anger.

"I just heard that you're moving to another park. What the hell Sarah? Did you think you could leave without telling me?" he scoffed, his voice filled with condemnation.

"Who did you hear that from?" His belittling tone of voice irritated me.

"I heard David talking with someone named Benjamin. What park are you going to? Why didn't you tell me yourself? Why did I have to overhear someone else's conversation?" His voice was full of accusations and hurt.

I bit my tongue as irritation simmered within me. "Warren, I don't owe you anything." I hissed between clenched teeth. "It's over between us! We're done. I... don't... owe... you... anything!"

He closed the gap between us, reaching for my arms. "Come on, Sarah. One last time, before you go."

My anger flared, and I pushed him away firmly. "No, Warren! I've said it's over! I want nothing to do with you anymore! Get away from me and leave me alone!"

Much like Virginia's persistence with Hudson, Warren refused to accept my rejection. The conversation quickly escalated into a tense and heated exchange. My temper flared and I finally had enough.

I took a deep breath. "If you don't leave right now, I swear to you, I'll file an assault charge against you! You need to leave now!"

Anger flashed in Warren's eyes, and he took a menacing step toward me. My heart raced faster than a heavy metal drum solo. I wasn't expecting him to get aggressive, and panic surged through me. I tried backing away, but he grabbed my arms and pulled me closer to him.

Trying to push him away from me was impossible, he was just too strong. Desperation filled me as we struggled. Tears filled my eyes and ran down my face. I could feel my pulse pounding in my temples and my voice rose as I screamed, "No!"

I'd never been afraid of Warren before, but I was now. His crazed look was something out of a psychological thriller movie. I was afraid for my life. Just as he moved closer to force a kiss onto me, I screamed 'no' and turned my head. A loud pounding sounded from my door, distracting Warren.

Warren whipped around as the door jamb cracked and the door flew open. Two rangers I barely knew busted in and pulled Warren away from me. He may have been stronger than me, but he was no match for the two men.

The wild look in Warren's eyes and rapid breathing were something I'd never seen before, and I hoped I'd never see it again. It was as if he was a deranged, wild beast ready to unleash years of pent-up fury all at once at me.

Soon, a crowd began to gather. A few were even recording what was happening with their phones. The rangers, who were holding Warren, pushed him to the ground and fought to move his arms behind him.

David shoved his way past the small crowd blocking the door. "Those videos had better not make it to the Internet, or I'll fire you so fast your heads won't have time to spin!" David stated in a firm tone and walked over to me, reaching for me. I flinched and pulled back.

My heart was still racing, and I was shaking like a leaf in a hurricane. My hands felt cold, and I couldn't catch my breath. I needed to get out of here!

I could see David's lips moving but I couldn't hear anything come out of his mouth. David's soothing voice finally reached me. "... safe now. No one's going to hurt you."

David handed me a bottle of water, but I was shaking so badly, and my hands weren't working properly. He opened the bottle and handed it back to me. Taking a sip, I watched as two rangers practically carried Warren away in cuffs.

David stood beside me; his presence was a calming influence after the chaos that had just unfolded. I tried to steady my breathing, but my heart still raced, and my hands still trembled.

"Take your time, Sarah," he said in a soothing tone. "You're safe now, and we'll sort this out."

I nodded, trying to find my voice. "I can't believe Warren would do something like that," I stammered, my voice still shaky.

David placed a reassuring hand on my shoulder. "I know it's shocking, Sarah, but you handled the situation well. Depending on what was caught on camera, you may only need to sign an affidavit swearing to your account of what happened. If that's the case, you could leave for your next post a few days early. I'll find out and let you know."

Tears welled up in my eyes, not from fear this time, but from the relief of knowing that there was at least some evidence to support my side of the story.

After a few hours of waiting, David had managed to review the video evidence, and to my relief, more had been captured than I initially thought. Someone in the crowd had been recording, and another had rushed to get help when the situation escalated. The presence of audio before the door was forced open added an important layer to the evidence against Warren.

I sat down to write the affidavit, detailing the events as accurately as I could recall. The prosecuting attorney assured me that they would take it from there. Warren, in all likelihood, would end up with a record and a fine, but there wouldn't be much, or any, jail time involved depending on Warren's attorney. According to the prosecuting attorney, in the grand scheme of things, this incident didn't rank as a significant offense. The best part, as far as I was concerned, was that Warren would be fired and more importantly, wouldn't ever be able to work in any national park ever again.

# Chapter Twelve

Sarah

My tires crunched over the gravel road as I approached Hudson's campground again. The drive had been long, and exhaustion hung heavy on my shoulders. I couldn't wait to settle in for a good night's rest.

The familiar landscape of towering pines and the scent of the forest filled my senses as I pulled into the campground. Hudson had been kind enough to offer me the same cabin at a highly discounted rate until my job started and I could move into the ranger housing. He'd told me I could stay for no charge, but I couldn't do that to him. I found a vacant space, parked my car, and shut off the engine.

With a tired sigh, I stepped out of the car and stretched my stiff muscles. The journey had been draining, but I was finally back in a place that felt like home. I walked over to the small porch of my cabin and set my bags down, taking a moment to breathe in the crisp, pine-scented air.

As I opened the door and stepped inside, an unexpected wave of nostalgia washed over me. The cozy cabin was just as I remembered it, filled with the rustic charm that had drawn me to this place in the first place. I knew I'd miss this cabin when I moved into ranger housing.

I unpacked my essentials and changed into more comfortable clothes. I considered making myself a cup of coffee but decided that sleep was a more pressing need. I crawled into the inviting warmth of the bed, exhaustion lulling me into a deep, dreamless slumber.

Tomorrow would be a new day, and I looked forward to reuniting with Hudson and exploring the Black Hills National Park more thoroughly. And wear appropriate shoes while doing it.

After a good night's sleep, I enjoyed a refreshing shower. I'd just finished dressing in comfortable clothes when I heard a familiar knock on the cabin door. A warm anticipation filled me as I approached, hoping it was Hudson. I opened the door, and he greeted me with a tight hug and a sweet kiss that made my heart skip a beat.

Hudson's touch was comforting, and I welcomed him inside the cabin. As we settled on the small couch, I began to recount the unsettling encounter with Warren. Hudson's expression darkened with anger as I spoke, his jaw clenched in frustration. I gently placed a hand on his arm, coaxing him to calm down.

"Just take a deep breath, Hudson," I urged softly. "He's not worth getting worked up over. I'm okay, and that's what matters."

Hudson nodded, and his anger slowly subsided. He leaned in, and I felt the familiar pull between us as we were about to share a kiss. Just then, there was another knock on the door. We chuckled, assuming it was James, and we both said his name in unison. I shook my head, not believing his uncanny timing again.

But as Hudson answered the door, no one was there. His forehead creased in confusion, and I couldn't help but laugh at the strange turn of events. Then, his gaze landed on an envelope placed deliberately on the doormat.

Hudson picked it up, and I watched as his eyes scanned the message it contained. It was a handwritten note that read:

> "Within the depths of your land, secrets untold,
> Hidden treasures await, glimmering gold.
> Beneath the tall pines and starry night's gleam,
> Embark on this quest, fulfill your dream."

I couldn't believe my ears as Hudson read aloud the mysterious message, and my curiosity piqued. What kind of treasure could be hidden on his land, and who had left this enigmatic note? It seemed like an adventure was about to unfold, and I couldn't wait to see where it would lead us.

Hudson and I sat down on the couch, the mysterious message in his hand drawing our attention. We pondered over its origins and meaning. It felt like something straight out of an adventure novel.

"I can't believe James would pull a stunt like this," I said, leaning closer to get a better look at the note. "But then again, he does have an affinity for inter... surprising us. Not always in a good way though," I said with a grin.

Hudson nodded in agreement. "You might be onto something there. This does seem like one of James's elaborate jokes."

As we debated whether or not to embark on this treasure hunt, we couldn't deny the excitement bubbling within us. The idea of exploring his land in search of hidden treasures was undeniably appealing. However, we both understood that one cryptic note was hardly enough to start a serious quest.

Later in the day, as the sun began to dip below the horizon, another note mysteriously appeared. It was as if it had materialized out of thin air, sitting on the cabin table. We exchanged glances, our curiosity piqued once more.

This new note provided a starting point, presenting us with longitude and latitude coordinates. With a sense of anticipation, Hudson and I entered the coordinates into our phones, eager to see where they would lead. We arrived at the specified location, surrounded by the beauty of the area, but it soon became clear that we needed more information to make sense of our surroundings.

Disappointed but undeterred, we returned to the campground as dusk settled in. We were determined to crack the code and uncover the hidden treasure, even if it meant decoding the intricate drawings and meanings on the next note, which we had decided to tackle the following day. The adventure was just beginning, and we couldn't wait to see where it would take us.

My morning began with the gentle rustling of leaves outside my cabin window, reminding me of the beautiful natural surroundings I had become a part of. As I got ready for the day, a soft knock on my cabin door interrupted my thoughts. I quickly finished buttoning my jeans and went to answer it.

To my delight, Hudson stood there with a mischievous glint in his eyes. He held out a note with a mysterious smile. "Good morning," he greeted me with a warm hug and kiss.

I returned the smile and took the note from him. As I unfolded it, my eyes scanned the words and images, and I began to read aloud,

> "The first note was just to see,
> If treasure hunting interests thee.
> Now it's time to start the quest,
> Search for the symbols and do your best."

I looked up at Hudson, puzzled but intrigued. "What the heck is that supposed to mean?"

Hudson chuckled, "It means the treasure hunt has officially begun. We need to head to the location mentioned on this note and look for symbols drawn on the third note."

"Did you know James was this clever? He's really put some thought into this." I remarked, genuinely impressed by his ingenuity.

"Honestly, no. But I'm glad he's upping his game. When we solve this, will you help me with something like this for him?" he asked with a hopeful smile.

I nodded, a sense of excitement and adventure bubbling within me. "Let's get started then. I can't wait to see where this leads us."

Hudson grinned, and together, we set off on our treasure hunt, ready to embrace the mysteries and challenges of this game.

Back at the starting point, Hudson and I scoured the area, searching for any sign of the symbols mentioned in the latest note. We inspected rocks, trees, and the ground, but nothing seemed to even come close to matching the images we received.

Frustration began to creep in as we realized that the clues weren't leading us to an obvious answer. I looked around in hopes of finding something, anything, that might help us decipher this puzzle.

Then, as I sat under a tall tree, my eyes wandered upward, scanning the branches above. And there, about twenty feet off the ground, on the underside of a thick limb, I saw something that could be one of the symbols. My heart skipped a beat.

"Hudson!" I called out, my voice filled with excitement. "Look up there! Do you see that?"

He followed my gaze and squinted at the object in question. "Yeah, I see it. But how on earth did James get up there, and why would he carve it under the limb?"

Those were excellent questions and ones that I couldn't answer from my vantage point on the ground. Determined to investigate further, I turned to Hudson. "Can you give me a leg up? Maybe I can reach the nearest branch, and we can go from there."

He nodded and crouched down, offering me his cupped hands. I stepped onto his palms and felt myself being lifted off the ground. With his help, I managed to grab the lowest branch. Slowly, I pulled myself up, my muscles straining with the effort.

As I reached the branch where the symbol was carved, I inspected it as closely as I could. To my surprise, the carving appeared old and weathered, not freshly made. It left me with even more questions than answers, but it was one of the symbols.

"If I drop my phone, catch it!" I called down to him. Straddling the sturdy branch, I reversed the camera direction on my phone and carefully slid it under the limb. It took a few tries to get it right, but once I was satisfied with the picture, I made my way down the tree. Hanging from the lowest branch, I dropped to the forest floor. Hudson caught me, slowing my descent.

"Thank you for that," I said as I turned around. Reaching up, I rested my hand on his cheek and stood on my toes. Damn! I was still too short. Hudson leaned down and kissed me. His soft lips pressed against mine and all I wanted to do was stay like that a little longer, but a loud sound made me jump.

My heartbeat sped up, but Hudson leaned in and said reassuringly, "Don't worry, Sarah. It's probably just a small rockslide. We're safe here. The hills can cause sounds to echo off each other, making it sound closer than it actually is."

I laughed uncomfortably. As my racing heart gradually slowed down, we focused on the picture of the symbol I'd discovered. It had been roughly carved into the underside of the branch, and it resembled an elongated diamond shape with a series of interconnected lines forming a simple pattern within it.

Studying the symbol, we realized it didn't match anything in the key. An understanding struck us — the mark we'd found was a combination of two different symbols. The diamond shape indicated treasure and the lines indicated distance, but it still wasn't enough.

I took a deep breath. "Maybe we should see if we can find any other symbols."

Hudson nodded in agreement, his eyes scanning the surrounding trees. "You're right. We need more pieces of the puzzle to figure this out. Let's keep looking and see if we can find anything else."

Hudson and I continued our search for more symbols, exploring the branches up in the trees around us. It didn't take us long to discover two additional carvings. With Hudson's assistance, I climbed the trees to reach the symbols, ready to clearly capture every detail, no matter how many tries it took.

The second symbol was a simple circle with three short lines radiating outward from its center, it reminded me of a child's drawing of a sun on the horizon. The third symbol was a zigzag pattern with three horizontal lines intersecting it at different points.

According to the key, the circle with three lines radiating from the center indicated direction, the zigzag indicated a trail, and the three lines indicated locations.

We continued to search the trees around us for any more symbols, but it seemed that the ones we had found were the only ones in this area. We exchanged glances, coming to the conclusion that it might mean a trail we needed to follow.

"We should look for a trail," I suggested. "It's possible that these symbols are guiding us along a specific path."

Hudson nodded in agreement. "I know a trail nearby that zigzags up a small mountain. I've been on it before, and it matches the pattern we've seen. We should check it out, but it's not a short trail. Before we do that, we need to be better supplied. You know, food, water, a tent, sleeping bags... just in case."

# Chapter Thirteen

Hudson

As Sarah and I returned to the campground, the sun was dipping below the horizon, casting long shadows over the serene landscape. We had originally planned to pack our backpacks and head out immediately, but the fading daylight made us reconsider.

"It's getting late," I remarked, my voice tinged with concern. "I think it would be safer to start fresh in the morning. We don't want to get caught in the wilderness after dark unprepared."

"Agreed. Besides, it's been a long day," Sarah added with a smile.

I walked Sarah to her cabin, and just as we reached her door, we discovered another message. It was partially concealed beneath the doormat. I retrieved it and read the rhyme aloud to Sarah. Excitement and curiosity were building within us.

> "The kiss they shared was oh so sweet,
> In their love, they're truly complete.
> But now it's time for a quest so grand,
> To find the treasure, they must understand."
> "Congratulations on the symbols you've found,
> Yet hidden secrets still abound.

> Are you sure you've found them all?
> Prepare for a journey, both big and small."
> "In the morning's light, your adventure will sweeten,
> With every step, let the mystery deepen.
> Follow the clues, let your hearts be your guide,
> And in the end, treasure you'll see inside."
> "Sleep well tonight, for a new day awaits,
> With challenges and mysteries at the gates.
> The path to riches, together you'll chase,
> In the heart of the Black Hills, at a thrilling pace."

"Okay, I'm officially creeped out." Sarah looked at me, her eyes filled with unease.

I didn't think that James was capable of crafting such elaborate rhymes. One or two lines, okay sure, but an entire poem? The realization that we were being watched, whoever it was, was getting inside our heads.

I offered, "If you're not comfortable staying alone tonight, you can stay with me. We'll lock up tight, and I'll make sure nothing happens. Plus, James will be there too. The more, the safer."

Her relief was evident as she nodded. "I'd really appreciate that. I can't shake this feeling of being watched now."

Sarah packed her bag with her things, and we went to my RV. After locking up the RV securely, we sat at the table. I noticed the subtle trembling in Sarah's hands. Her eyes held a trace of fear that hadn't fully dissipated since we found that message. James emerged from his bedroom, and the air tensed as Sarah, and I looked at each other.

We questioned James about the notes. He seemed genuinely surprised and denied any involvement. He explained that he had gone into Custer today for lunch and wandered around afterward. James even offered to show us the credit card receipt from the restaurant as proof of his whereabouts, but I waved it off. I believed him.

James proposed to go with us tomorrow, but just as we were about to accept, he received a call.

"Hey Tom... What?... That can't be... No, of course, I'll head that way tomorrow... Okay, see you then."

James sighed as he looked at Sarah and me. "I'm really sorry, guys," he began, "but this emergency at work, it's a big deal. I've got to pack as much as I can tonight and load up the car. I have to leave early in the morning and won't be able to help you with the treasure hunt, but honestly, maybe you shouldn't go after all."

I could see the concern in his eyes, genuine worry for our safety. It gave me pause, and I exchanged a glance with Sarah, silently contemplating our next move.

As James went about packing and loading his car, doubt gnawed at us. Sarah and I traded worried looks, contemplating whether we should continue with this or not.

I wondered how much stuff he brought in the first place. After several trips in and out of the RV, helping James load his belongings, only his suitcase would need to be packed tomorrow. I watched as James took a moment to catch his breath, his expression serious and concerned. It was clear he didn't want us to go alone, but the urgency of his work situation had to take priority.

James retreated to his room, leaving us alone at the table. I put my arm around Sarah's waist, drawing her closer to me. The weight of uncertainty hung in the air as we considered the treasure hunt and the unknown watcher who seemed to be orchestrating this game.

We whispered in hushed tones, contemplating the risks and rewards. But our conversation was abruptly interrupted when an unexpected knock on the door jolted us. Nerves got the best of us, and we shared a nervous laugh before I made my way to answer the door.

As I swung it open, a piece of paper fluttered down from above, narrowly escaping my grasp. I quickly bent down to retrieve it. It was another poem. I scanned the contents. My brow furrowed as I read the note.

"Okay, that doesn't look good. What does it say?" Sarah asked, worry in her tone.

"In the shadows, secrets bide,
A warning for you, don't let them hide.

> The treasure's path, you must tread,
> Or darkness looms, danger ahead."
> "A choice you face, to venture on,
> Or risk the night, 'til hope is gone.
> The clock ticks, the hour's late,
> Hunt the treasure or seal your fate!"

"I don't know anyone who can come up with a rhyme that fast," Sarah whispered so softly, that I could barely hear her.

I leaned in close, my lips brushing against Sarah's ear as I whispered, "You're right, that was too fast. We're being watched and listened to." I pulled back slightly, my gaze locking with hers as I added quietly, "We'll have to be careful about what we say."

Out loud, I asked, "What happens if we don't go?"

A few moments later, another knock at the door sent a shiver down my spine. I quickly retrieved the new note and read the ominous rhyme.

> "In the dark of night, beware the fire's might,
> A raging tempest, a fearsome sight.
> If you stay behind, your fate will be dire,
> For flames shall consume, a relentless pyre."
> "To the mountains high, you must take flight,
> Or in this inferno, you'll face your plight.
> A choice to make, with haste and care,
> For if you stay, it's danger's snare."
> "With every passing hour, the flames grow near,
> So heed this warning, make no delay here.
> To save your souls, you must be fast,
> Or in the flame's grip, will be your last!"
> "In the morning, you must start early,
> To continue on, and start your journey.
> "Don't test me now, it's your time to learn.
> Flames consume, and all will burn!"

"Is this saying that whoever is doing this will burn down the forest or your campground?" Sarah asked, her voice trembling, as if the thought of the forest and my campground going up in flames was inconceivable.

We leaned in close, our voices barely above a whisper as we discussed our decision to follow the clues. I could feel my own unease reflected in Sarah's teary eyes, and I couldn't shake the nervousness coursing through me.

I cleared my throat and spoke aloud. "All right, it's getting late. We've got an early day tomorrow," I said, my voice slightly unsteady. "We'll follow the clues."

We entered my bedroom and Sarah went into the bathroom to prepare for bed. I took the opportunity to turn my computer on to find some music to play while we were in here. Something that had a frequency. Something that would hopefully interfere with whatever they were using to listen to us. The soothing sounds of rain and thunder filled the room, and I tried to relax, but the weight of the situation pressed heavily on me.

Sarah emerged from the bathroom, looking sexy in her pajamas, a soft smile on her face. She wore a shapely set of matching shorts and a tank top with a subtle floral pattern. If it weren't for James, whoever is listening, and the threat...

I got up from the bed, wrapping my arms around her for a warm hug, and placed a gentle kiss on her forehead. "I'll be quick," I reassured her before slipping into the bathroom. When I emerged, I was dressed in my own pajamas, a comfortable set of navy blue cotton pants, and a plain white T-shirt.

We climbed into bed, side by side, but the weight of impending danger kept us both restless. We tossed and turned, the worry and uncertainty making it difficult to fall asleep.

Finally, exhaustion took over, and I pulled Sarah close, wrapping my arms around her. We clung to each other, seeking comfort in each other's embrace. The rhythmic sound of our breathing lulled us to sleep. Regardless of the looming threat that lay ahead, I reveled in our closeness, and my last thoughts before sleep took me to where there was a future with Sarah.

The first rays of the morning sun gently filtered through the window shades. I heard James up and about as he got ready to leave. Reluctantly, I got out of bed, the comforting warmth of Sarah's body next to mine left me and all I wanted to do was get back in bed with her.

I entered the kitchen area and sat at the table. James sat down and I told him to drive carefully and send a text to let me know he made it okay. I decided against telling him about the problem last night, we hugged, and James left. He didn't need to get involved in this mess.

I released a heavy sigh, my thoughts were weighed down like the coffee grounds in the filter drowning in scalding hot water. What had started as a potentially exciting treasure hunt now felt shrouded in foreboding darkness, casting an ominous shadow over our plans. The thrill of the adventure had been replaced by a gnawing sense of impending danger.

As the coffee maker completed its task, I poured myself a cup, the fragrant aroma filling the RV. Carefully adding creamer, I stirred the light brown concoction, my mind adrift in a sea of thoughts. Time seemed to blur, and before I knew it, Sarah emerged from the bedroom, fully prepared for the day ahead.

"Good morning," I said. My attempt at cheerfulness didn't match my true feelings.

"Good morning. Any coffee pods left?" Sarah asked; her demeanor noticeably brighter than mine.

"Absolutely," I replied, forcing a smile. "I'll make you a cup. Please, have a seat."

I set the coffee cup in front of Sarah and reached for a paper napkin to place beside it. Just as I was about to set it down, a sharp knock echoed through the RV, startling me. The napkin slipped from my fingers and fluttered to the floor. Sarah bent to pick it up while I went to answer the door.

Opening the door, my eyes fell upon another note. Another note and another rhyme. I read it aloud.

> "Now that James has left and gone,
> It's time for you to carry on.
> Seek the treasure, find the maze,
> Before the forest's set ablaze."

Sarah shot me a meaningful glance and placed a finger against her lips, shushing me. She held up her hand, palm up, and pretended to write on it. I grabbed a pen and pad of paper and placed them in her waiting hand.

While she wrote on the paper, she said, "While you get ready to leave, I'll pack, and we can go."

She handed the note to me, and my eyes widened in alarm as I read about the listening device beneath the table. A surge of anger welled up inside me, causing my jaw to clench tightly.

"Yeah," I grumbled, struggling to contain my frustration. "Let me finish my coffee, and then I'll get ready to go." My rage simmered just beneath the surface.

I sat in the chair beside Sarah, the lingering tension from the discovery of the listening device still filling my mind. We both took slow sips of our coffee as if the ritual of a morning brew could, at least for now, chase away our worries.

We avoided speaking about the bug hidden under the table and the unavoidable hunt for more clues. Instead, we granted ourselves a short break from the darkness threatening what we held dear, finding comfort in the simple, everyday moments of a morning together.

As I stepped into the bathroom to get ready, my mind raced with a whirlwind of questions about the mysterious events unfolding around us. The 'whys' and 'hows' churned in my thoughts like elusive shadows. I hurriedly went through my morning routine, hoping to shake off the anxiety that had settled in.

When I was finally ready, I left the bathroom and returned to the kitchen. Sarah had packed two backpacks. Without a word, we helped each other put on a backpack, adjusting the belts and straps, and we left the RV. I held out my hand to Sarah and she took it as we headed back to where it started.

# Chapter Fourteen

Sarah

Hudson extended his hand, and I gratefully accepted it, feeling the warmth and security it provided. Together, we set off on the hike to retrace our steps toward the trees where we had discovered those symbols. The path led us further, and it felt as though we were venturing into a tunnel of trees, their branches leaning over the trail, almost as if they were reaching out to each other.

Cautiously, we ascended the trail, which seemed to be heading toward a nearby mountain. The rocky terrain underfoot made the trek difficult, and Hudson commented on how he didn't remember it being quite this rocky before. I chuckled and replied, "I'm just grateful my ankle is healed now."

We stopped beside the trees along the way that matched the symbol, our gazes turning upward in search of more of the strange symbols. Hudson noticed one of them and I climbed the tree to take the picture.

This symbol was a double arrow, the arrows pointed in opposite directions. The key stated that a choice would need to be made further up the path.

As Hudson and I continued up the zigzagging trail, we stumbled upon the spots that seemed to correspond to the other locations hinted at by the intersecting lines on the zigzag symbol. It was in those two other places that we spotted two more symbols carved into the underside of the tree's branches.

The next one was a spiral, spiraling outward from the center. It meant the journey would not be straight. The third symbol we discovered was a curved arrow, resembling a crescent moon with a single line curving inward. It indicated a hidden path.

Hudson and I stood at the crossroads of our journey, believing we understood the meanings of the symbols we'd uncovered but still feeling lost in the puzzle's complexity. As we continued to walk, the symbols danced in my thoughts, and we discussed their potential significance.

"This treasure hunt has turned into an ordeal. And just think, when we first found out about it, we thought it would be fun. Who knew?" I remarked, my voice laced with sarcasm and apprehension.

Hudson nodded, his eyes focused on the path ahead. "True, but it feels like we're on the right track now. What I want to know is, who's our rhyming "friend," and why us?"

Deep in thought, I furrowed my brow. "I don't know. Maybe this is all just a really bad joke on us. I don't know, but we need to figure out which one leads to the treasure... if there really is a treasure."

Our conversation paused as we reached a point where the trail split into three partially hidden paths. We decided to start with the first one, but it proved to be disappointingly straight and seemingly endless. After retracing our steps, we tried the second path, which curved intriguingly but eventually led us to a dead end.

Frustration nagged at us, but we kept our spirits up as we ventured down the third path, which meandered and wound its way uphill. It felt different from the other two, but it seemed like it had a purpose, and we exchanged hopeful glances.

"This trail seems right," Hudson said, his voice optimistic.

We continued along the winding path until it abruptly ended at a steep ravine. On the other side, we spotted what appeared to be a continuation of the trail, but the gap between us and the opposite side was significant.

I turned to Hudson, and we exchanged concerned looks. "How are we going to cross this?" My concern was mirrored in his eyes as we stood at the edge of the ravine, assessing our options.

Hudson voiced his thoughts, "Rappelling down is doable, but getting back up could be a problem. Plus, we don't have the right gear or shoes for that."

I nodded in agreement. "Rappelling down a cliff without the proper equipment is too risky. We have some rope with us, but not nearly enough for a descent or ascent. Plus, I've never done any climbing before. And I don't think now is the time to learn."

"Yeah, not a good time," he agreed.

After a few moments of contemplation, we both seemed to reach a silent consensus. I finally spoke up, "I don't want to take any unnecessary risks. We can try walking up the ravine and hope we can find a natural bridge or a spot where we can jump across safely. What do you think?"

Hudson nodded, and we began our trek, walking beside the ravine, hoping that our decision would lead us to a solution and keep us safe.

"I know the Black Hills are supposedly full of lost gold treasures, but no one ever seems to find them. You know, if there really is a treasure… well… have you heard about this one before?" I asked, my curiosity aroused.

Hudson shared stories of lost or hidden gold bullion, dust, bars, coins, and jewelry, even mentioning silver coins hidden in South Dakota. He explained that while the legends spoke of these treasures, they were often located far from where we currently were. But he also added, "Even if someone did stumble on something, they could never seem to find the spot again, and they were usually in pretty bad shape when they returned."

A few hours passed as we continued on through rocky and wooded areas, and we finally found a place where we could safely jump across the ravine. With a shared sigh of relief, we landed on the other side and made our way back to the trail. The sun was sinking low on the horizon, casting long shadows through the trees, and we decided that it was time to set up camp for the night.

Once our campsite was ready, we needed to gather some firewood. With backpacks and flashlights in hand, we ventured into the surrounding forest, searching for dry branches and twigs to fuel our fire. The woods seemed eerily quiet as night fell, with only the rustling of leaves and the distant chirping of crickets breaking the silence.

When we returned to camp with a bundle of firewood, we were greeted by an unexpected sight. There, where we'd placed rocks to contain the fire we were going to build, lay a note. Hudson picked it up, and his brow furrowed as he read aloud,

> "In twilight's hush, a message to hear,
> "Wasting time," it whispers clear.
> Through the woods, you wandered wide,
> Misused your time, you need to decide."
> "Flickering flames light your quest,
> In this adventure, you're put to the test.
> With hearts resolved, you journey on,
> Through starlit paths till the dawn."

"Is that supposed to mean we shouldn't rest? That's just stupid!" Hudson angrily huffed.

I exchanged puzzled glances with him. "Agreed, but how did this get here?" I asked, my voice filled with confusion and a hint of unease.

Hudson shook his head, clearly just as baffled as I was. "I have no idea, Sarah. It's like someone is always one step ahead of us."

We set the note aside, my thoughts filled with a growing sense of foreboding. Despite our uncertainties, we knew that we had to continue this treasure hunt, whether we liked it or not.

The night settled in around us, the crackling campfire was the only source of warmth and light. We enjoyed our simple dinner and with exhaustion slowly creeping in, retreated to our tent, ready to rest our weary bodies.

As we settled into our sleeping bags, a distant whirring sound disrupted the tranquility. It grew louder, approaching rapidly. I unzipped the tent flap, and we both emerged to see a small drone hovering above us.

Its mechanical propellers buzzed with an unnerving intensity, and it descended to the ground with a soft thud. Before our astonished eyes, it placed a note on the ground and, without delay, soared away, disappearing across the dark ravine.

The note bore a stern message, a rhyme forcefully demanding us to break camp and continue onward, as if a relentless force urged us to hasten our quest, leaving us with a sense of unease.

> "Break camp now, no time to rest,
> In shadows, danger's lurking quest.
> The night conceals what's yet unknown,
> Onward, on your journey, you must be shown."
> "The path ahead, a winding thread,
> Through darkness and what lies ahead.
> With every step, the truth unfolds,
> Keep moving forward, you must be bold."

From the edge of the ravine, Hudson's voice echoed across the dark expanse. His frustration was evident as he yelled out, "It's dark, we're tired, and we need rest! If we continue on tonight and something happens to us, you're as screwed as we are!"

I stood beside him, my weariness matching his own. The tension hung heavy in the night air as we waited for a response from the unseen sender of the notes, hoping for a moment of reprieve.

The distant whirring of the drone returned, and I watched anxiously as it descended, delivering yet another note. It was a persistent reminder that our every move was being watched, our every step dictated by an unseen hand.

I unfolded the note, and its rhyme read with a firm tone:

> "In the morn, when day's first light,
> Set forth on your quest, don't delay the flight.
> The treasure's there, but time won't wait,
> Break camp at dawn, it's your appointed fate."

The weight of the situation pressed upon us, and I couldn't help but wonder what lay ahead as we prepared to face a new day and the challenges it held.

As Hudson and I stood there, the drone's distant buzz faded into the night, and we couldn't shake the unsettling feeling that had settled upon us like a heavy shroud. I turned to him, my voice filled with frustration and curiosity.

"Why all these rhymes? It's as if someone is playing... just... ludicrous games with us," I muttered, my brows furrowing.

Hudson ran a hand through his hair, his expression tense. "I wish I knew. It's like they're taunting us, pushing us to continue. But why? And who's behind all of this?"

We exchanged a troubled glance; it was as if our unanswered questions were hanging in the air like an irritating mosquito. The only certainty was that we were deep in a mystery we couldn't yet fathom, and with each rhyme, the enigma only seemed to deepen.

The night in the tent had been colder than expected, with our thoughts lingering on the mysterious drone operator and the bizarre rhymes. Hudson and I had snuggled closer for warmth, seeking comfort in each other's arms. Eventually, fatigue claimed us, and we drifted into a fitful sleep.

Morning arrived with an unwelcome drone's hum, jolting us awake. There was no note this time, just a cruel wake-up call from our unseen pursuer. As we emerged from the tent, the drone swiftly departed, leaving us with a sense of unease.

We broke camp, preparing to continue our quest. While we packed our belongings, Hudson and I found ourselves delving into more personal conversations, perhaps as a way to temporarily escape the strange circumstances that surrounded us. Our voices filled the crisp morning air as we shared stories, hopes, and dreams, a small island of normalcy in the midst of a bewildering mission.

We helped each other secure our backpacks, and with our gear in place, we resumed the ascent, following the trail. The landscape around us was breathtaking, an untouched part of Hudson's land that he told me he'd never explored before.

As we continued, Hudson opened up about his family. He explained that he owned 127 acres of this vast wilderness, bequeathed to him in his grandfather's will. And no, he didn't actually have to save the money to buy it. He said that it's just easier to tell people that. I didn't understand why, but it's his life. He also told me that in order to fund the construction of the campground, he'd sold off 10 acres.

"Grandpa left James a business to run. No matter how he acts, he's very business savvy. Since he took over five years ago, his ideas have expanded the company and nearly doubled sales for them."

"That's impressive. You're right though, he doesn't act like a businessman. But I guess he was supposed to be on vacation."

Our hike eventually led us to a formidable rock face that seemed devoid of clues. Perplexed, I took a seat on a large rock nestled against the imposing stone wall, with a few bushes beside it. Suddenly, a chilled breeze pushed against me, making me jump in surprise.

"Are you okay?" Hudson rushed to my side.

"I wasn't expecting that. I guess I'm slightly jumpy," I said a little embarrassed.

# Chapter Fifteen

### Hudson

"I wasn't expecting that. I guess I'm slightly jumpy," Sarah softly laughed, looking nervous and brushing a strand of hair from her face.

"What happened?" I asked, my voice edged with concern.

She cocked her head to the side as she stared at the rock she'd been sitting on. "Check this out," she said waving me over to her.

There was a small opening in the rock face, partially hidden by the bushes and the rock. I bent down to get a better look and noticed a symbol roughly carved into the stone. We'd seen this symbol before. It was a circle with three lines radiating from the center, pointing toward the rock.

I watched as Sarah squeezed herself through the small opening in the rock face. She seemed to slip inside effortlessly, disappearing from view. I couldn't help but feel a twinge of unease as I waited outside, the uncertainty of what lay beyond that narrow entrance nagged at me.

"Sarah, are you okay in there?" I called out, my voice teeming with apprehension.

Her muffled response echoed back to me from within the rock, "I'm fine, Hudson. It's a bit tight, but I can manage. I'll let you know what I find."

I remained outside, my worry growing with each passing moment. I continued to talk with Sarah, our voices serving as a lifeline connecting us through the rocky barrier.

I listened anxiously to Sarah's muffled echoing from inside the cave. Her words reached me, filling me with both relief and a lingering sense of worry. "There's a cavern in here, about ten feet or so. I'm going to explore it."

I hesitated for a moment, torn between wanting to follow her inside and my concerns about the tight opening. But ultimately, I trusted her judgment. "Okay, be careful in there, Sarah. Keep talking to me and let me know if you find anything unusual."

I sat down, keeping my attention focused on her voice, hoping that she would soon reveal clues about the treasure we were hunting for and get out of there as soon as possible.

As I waited outside the cave, the persistent whirring of the drone returned, breaking the silence of the forest. Frustration and suspicion churned within me. Without hesitation, I picked up a small stone and sent it flying toward the hovering drone and then shot the bird at it. It retreated quickly.

Moments later, I heard Sarah's voice, and my attention snapped back to the small opening. She emerged from the narrow passage, her face reflecting disappointment. "There wasn't much in the small cavern. Just another one of those circles with lines coming out of it. There's a tunnel, but it's too high up for me to reach and check if it goes anywhere."

The puzzle was growing more complicated, and the urgency to unravel its secrets weighed on us both. I wondered what lay beyond that inaccessible tunnel.

Sarah and I exchanged uncertain glances as we contemplated the narrow tunnel entrance. I voiced my concerns. "I'm not sure if I could fit inside or not. I'd really hate to get stuck anywhere in there."

"I'd hate for you to get stuck in there too. You could try and if there are any places where it's just too tight, you can back out. If needed, I can pull you out. At least it could help you move backward through the tighter places, but if you don't want to even try, it's okay. We'll figure something out," she said with a half-smile as she tipped her head to the side.

As we mulled over the possibility, the drone returned, interrupting our conversation. It landed, and I retrieved the note, curiosity building as I read the rhyme aloud,

> "Time is fleeting, don't you see?
> On this hunt, you must agree.
> The clues ahead, the path untrod,
> Don't stand still, continue to plod."

I leaned in close to Sarah, my voice a whisper. "I don't think the rhymer knows about the tunnel. It might be more about us not moving. We should check our gear for any trackers or bugs."

We thoroughly searched through our backpacks, and my heart sank when I discovered a GPS tracker among my belongings. Sarah, too, found one in her pack. There were no bugs, which was a small relief, but the presence of these trackers only deepened the mystery.

Sarah let out a sigh of relief. "At least we don't have to whisper anymore," she remarked, her voice carrying a bit more ease.

I couldn't help but smile at her comment. "You know, I kind of like whispering to you," I admitted, my voice softer as I looked into her eyes, hoping to ease more of the tension that still lingered.

"Does that mean you just like being that close to me?" Sarah glanced my way, a teasing smile playing on her lips, and I nodded in response.

I felt my heart skip a beat as I heard her words. "Good, because I like it too," she continued, her eyes locking onto mine with an intensity that sent a shiver down my spine. "And when this is over, I think we should do something about it."

"I think that's an excellent idea," I whispered, my voice filled with anticipation and desire. Leaning closer, I pressed my lips softly against hers. The kiss was tender, filled with longing and promise. She returned it, her hand finding its way to my racing heart, which seemed to beat in rhythm with the moment.

I didn't want the kiss to end; I wanted more. But as she pulled away, our eyes locked, and I could see the same desire in her expression that I was feeling.

"What are we going to do about the trackers? It's not like we can throw them away and I don't want to hang onto them either. I also want to know how and when it got in our packs in the first place." I was frustrated... in more than one way.

We decided to disarm one of the trackers and leave the other one untouched for now. I removed the battery from one of them and shoved it into one of my pockets and the tracker into the other.

Next was the challenge of the tunnel. The narrow opening seemed like it would be a very tight squeeze for me, but we needed to keep moving and find out where the other tunnel led. In case I got stuck, Sarah tied a rope to my ankle so that she could pull on it and help me to get back out.

The tunnel was tight, and I had to squirm my way in, inch by inch. My heart raced as I felt the walls pressing against me. It was tense and uncomfortable, but I continued. After what felt like an eternity, I emerged on the other side, relieved to have made it. Sarah followed and together we pulled the backpacks through.

As I lifted Sarah up to the entrance of the next tunnel, my thoughts briefly veered toward her weightlessness in my hands and the slender curve of her waist. I quickly brushed aside those distractions, focusing on the task at hand.

"All right, you ready for the packs?" I asked, our voices echoing faintly within the rocky confines.

"Yeah," she replied, her voice mingled with a hint of excitement.

I handed her the backpacks, and then, with a determined push, I pulled myself up into the tunnel. It was a relief to find this one somewhat more accommodating than the previous one, giving me a bit more breathing space.

We continued on, flashlights in hand, the underground environment feeling increasingly uncomfortable. The tunnel seemed longer than the first, but eventually, it opened up into a larger cavern. Our breaths echoed off the walls as we stood in awe of our surroundings.

As we ventured deeper into the cavern, our flashlights illuminated the mesmerizing world of stalactites and stalagmites, glistening like nature's intricate sculptures. A small pond lay in one corner, with water steadily dripping down from the ceiling, creating delicate ripples on its surface.

I marveled at the beauty surrounding us, though the air in the cavern had grown noticeably cooler. I wrapped my arm around Sarah, hoping to share some warmth.

"Look at those formations," she whispered in awe, her voice hushed in the underground expanse. "Did you have any idea this could be here?"

"No. They're amazing," I replied, our voices barely disturbing the tranquility.

The cavern was filled with a stunning array of mineral formations, each one was a silent witness to the intricate beauty of nature's stunning artwork.

Stalactites hung gracefully from the ceiling like frozen icicles, their slender forms tapering down to delicate points. Some were long and slender, while others formed intricate clusters, creating captivating patterns of draping formations. Their surfaces glistened with moisture, catching the beams of our flashlights and reflecting a shimmering, otherworldly glow.

Stalagmites, rising from the cave's floor, mirrored the stalactites above. They reached upward, their forms thinning as they grew taller, and some of them even met their counterparts from above, forming towering columns. Their bases displayed unique shapes, resembling frozen fountains or gnarled tree roots. Each one stretched upward in a slow and patient ascent toward the ceiling.

The colors of the formations varied, showing shades of white, gray, and delicate amber, with hints of translucent crystal. Each one was a tribute to the passage of time and the slow, steady work of water and minerals shaping the cave's interior into a breathtaking underground wonderland.

As our flashlights pierced through the darkness of the cavern, they conjured intricate and mysterious shadows on the ceilings, walls, and floor, enhancing the eerie beauty of the underground world.

The beams of light cast sharp, elongated shadows from the stalactites hanging above, creating a play of contrasts and forms that seemed to dance and sway with every movement. The shadows stretched and twisted, mimicking the shapes of the formations the flashlights shined on.

At times, the shadows would overlap, creating intricate patterns of darkness and light that seemed to tell stories of the cave's long history. The interplay of the cold, unyielding rock formations and the light of our flashlights lent the entire scene an almost surreal quality. It was as if we had stepped into a hidden realm untouched by the passage of time. The cavern felt alive, its shadows dancing to the rhythm of our exploration, leaving us in awe of this subterranean world.

Sarah, mindful of preserving nature's wonders, cautioned me, "Be careful not to touch them. The oils from our skin can harm these formations."

I nodded and we continued our exploration. As our flashlights danced across the cavern walls, we spotted another crude carving next to a tunnel, resembling something like a bar. We exchanged a puzzled glance, uncertain if it was a natural formation or a sign left behind by those who had been here before us.

We followed the tunnel; our flashlights pierced the darkness. My heart raced with excitement and apprehension. Within a small cavity in one of the walls was a smaller chest. It reminded me of a pirate's treasure chest. I nodded to Sarah, and she cautiously opened the chest, revealing slightly dusty but still gleaming coins.

I reached for one of the coins, it was heavy. The design featured a profile of a lady with the word Liberty across the band of her cap and stars surrounding her head. The year, eighteen thirty was at the bottom. The back had an eagle with a shield on its chest, its talons held three arrows and leaves. With the United States of America on its back, we were certain, this was what we'd been sent to find.

"That five D on the back, does that mean it's a five-dollar coin?" she asked, her tone filled with curiosity.

"I guess." My eyes remained fixed on the coins, their luster captivated me despite the layer of dust that clung to them.

"Oh God... What are we going to do? These coins are rightfully yours. We can't let whoever is out there pulling the strings to get them," she declared, her voice filled with worry.

# Chapter Sixteen

Sarah

We removed the coins from the metal chest. Some of the coins, particularly the ones with older dates, were slightly larger than the others. In total, there were fifty coins in the chest. But what caught our attention even more were the twelve gold bars hidden beneath the coins.

Each gold bar measured about six inches in length, three inches in width, and two inches in thickness. Their weight was substantial, and the sight of them left us in awe. It was a moment where we both realized the magnitude of what we had found in that hidden cavern.

I carefully returned the coins to their place in the chest, trying to get Hudson's attention. His gaze was fixed firmly on the gold treasure, and I had to touch his arm to bring him back to the present.

"We can't leave these here, and I don't think it's a good idea to carry them out. If the rhyming guy is out there, he could just take them from us," I said with concern in my voice. "What do you want to do?"

Hudson decided to hide the majority of the coins and bars in different locations within the cave to ensure their safety. He took pictures of the front and back of all the coins and bars. As he began to identify suitable hiding spots, I followed him, carefully placing the gold bars and coins in concealed nooks and crannies. It felt surreal as if we were part of some treasure-hunting adventure ourselves, even though the stakes were high and the mystery surrounding the rhyming notes still loomed over us.

We worked in silence, the weight of our discovery sinking in. Each hiding place was carefully chosen, and we made a mental note of their locations. It was a strange feeling, burying treasure deep within a cave, knowing that we might not be able to return to retrieve it for some time. And finally, the other tracker was smashed and shoved into one of my pockets.

After securing the majority of the coins and bars, we retrieved the chest with its remaining contents before we made our way back out of the cave. It was a calculated risk, but it seemed like the best course of action for the time being. With Hudson's newfound wealth hidden away, we retraced our steps and exited the tunnel.

After too many hours of work, I emerged from the tunnel into darkness, my heart racing with anxiety. Hudson followed closely behind, and as we stood once more in front of the cavern's mouth, relief washed over us. We retrieved the chest and our backpacks, carefully pulling them out of the tunnel with ropes.

But as we stepped out into the open air, the persistent whine of the drone filled our ears once more. We exchanged uneasy glances, realizing that our mysterious taskmaster had found us again. The drone descended, and with a sense of trepidation, we awaited the latest message.

> "To you dear seekers, a heartfelt thanks,
> For finding my treasure, through rocky banks.
> As dawn breaks free, your path is clear,
> Begin your trek and do not veer."
> "Now bring it back to the other side,
> Leave it there and continue your stride.
> The chest is heavy, your steps be sure,
> On your journey, do not detour."

We trudged back toward our campsite from last night. Even with both of us carrying the chest, its weight pulled down on us, and exhaustion descended like a dense fog. The once picturesque surroundings blurred into obscurity as our singular focus became reaching our previous location again.

Upon our arrival at the campsite, our bodies felt drained, every ounce of energy depleted by the strenuous journey and the weight we bore. The task of setting up the tent resembled a Herculean feat, our arms protesting every movement. Nevertheless, we pushed forward, and together we managed to raise the shelter. Crawling inside the tent, we surrendered to the overwhelming exhaustion and collapsed onto our sleeping bags.

As Hudson and I lay there, the exhaustion weighing us down like a ship's anchor, he let out a sigh. "I'm hungry," he mumbled, his voice heavy with fatigue.

I couldn't help but giggle, the sheer absurdity of our situation making me lightheaded. "Me too," I confessed, my laughter bubbling up. "But I'm too tired to move right now."

Hudson chuckled, his eyes twinkling with tired amusement. "What if you could have any meal you wanted right now, what would it be?"

I thought about it for a moment, and a smile played on my lips. "Pizza, with pepperoni, veggies, and lots of jalapenos," I declared, the words eliciting another round of laughter from both of us.

Hudson's tired eyes sparkled with humor. "Jalapenos? You like it spicy, huh?" he quipped, a faint smile tugging at his lips. "Pizza it is, half with jalapenos then. I don't think they deliver here. But for now, I think we'll have to settle for a well-deserved night's sleep. Getting the gold across the ravine is going to be interesting."

I awoke with a start, the sound of the drone, and it repeatedly colliding with the tent, assaulting my ears. The aches and pains from carrying the heavy gold the previous day made themselves vehemently known as I groggily tried to sit up.

Turning to Hudson, I couldn't help but mutter, "Do you think my arms will fall off, or is that just wishful thinking at this point?" The weight of the gold had taken its toll, and at that moment, the idea of no arms seemed strangely appealing.

He looked at me with a warm smile. "Don't worry, we're almost done with this mess," he said, his voice filled with reassurance. "Once we get back to my RV, I'll take care of those sore muscles for you. A massage might be just what you need after this."

Hudson's soothing voice brought a faint smile to my weary face. "A massage sounds like heaven right now," I admitted, "but we still have hours of carrying that chest left to go. By the time we get back, you may not feel like moving your arms at all. I'm positive I won't."

We discussed how we were going to carry the gold and Hudson suggested that we carry the gold in our backpacks. I agreed as we exited the tent. We'd left the chest outside of our tent so that whoever was watching us could keep an eye on it.

While I carried two bars and the ten coins, Hudson would carry four of the bars. It would still be too much to carry for me particularly, but at least not all the weight would be carried with our arms. Helping each other put the packs on was going to be a huge challenge, especially for me.

We loaded our backpacks with the gold, starting with Hudson's. It was a painstaking process, ensuring that the weight was distributed as evenly as possible. After I helped Hudson to put his pack on, he helped me with mine, making sure everything was secure and balanced on our shoulders and backs.

Just as we were about to set off, the persistent drone reappeared, and a new rhyme was delivered. The message read:

> "Take the chest, it goes with you,
> A crucial task that must ensue.
> Its weight, a symbol, your burden to bear,
> Don't test me now, the chest is quite rare."

As we trudged along the trail, the weight of our packs and the chest dragging us down and wearing us out, my mind was constantly on the rhyme sender. Hudson and I had been speculating about this mysterious figure ever since we found the first note. I decided to share my thoughts with him.

"Hudson," I began, my voice laced with curiosity, "do you think this person knows you? I mean, could it be someone from your past, like an old friend or maybe even a history teacher or professor?"

Hudson furrowed his brow, deep in thought. "It's possible," he replied, "but I've wracked my brain trying to come up with names or faces, and nothing concrete comes to mind. It's all just guesswork at this point."

We continued the hike, the weight of our silent contemplation heavy alongside the gold-laden packs. The identity of our rhyme sender remained shrouded in mystery, an enigma we were determined to solve as we navigated back to the point where we could cross back over.

As we reached the spot where we had jumped across the ravine to the side we were currently on, exhaustion weighed heavily upon us. My arms, legs, and back ached from the strain of carrying the chest and the gold, our breathing was labored, and every step felt like an arduous journey. It was clear that attempting to leap back over to the other side was out of the question; our packs were simply too heavy.

Hudson and I sat down, our chests heaving as we tried to catch our breath. We exchanged tired glances, knowing that a decision had to be made. I spoke, my voice strained but determined. "Hudson, we can't jump back over. These packs are too heavy. What do you think? Should we continue further up and see if there's another way to cross?"

Hudson, his face etched with weariness, nodded in agreement. "Sarah, you're right. We can't go back the way we came. Let's rest for a bit, gather our strength, and then we'll explore the area to see if there's another way across. We've come this far; we can't turn back now." With that decision made, we settled in for a brief rest.

With our packs removed, we sat at the edge of the ravine, trying to catch our breath. The drone returned, buzzing over our heads with only inches to spare. It hovered in front of us, drawing Hudson's rage.

"Can you hear me?" Hudson angrily bellowed. "Wiggle the camera if you can." To our amazement, the camera on the drone responded, tilting up and down.

Seizing the opportunity, Hudson began to explain our predicament to the drone operator on the other end. "Listen," he said, his tone earnest, "the gold we're carrying weighs more than Sarah and me combined. There's no way we can jump back across this ravine from here. If we continue further down and there's no way to cross, it's going to take us even longer. If you send the drone ahead, it could save time, and you'll get the gold and chest sooner."

With that plea, the operator seemed to understand our situation and the drone darted further down the path, its whirring propellers carrying it further from us and the sounds of nature surrounded us once more.

I laid back. "I don't think I can move anymore today. Everything hurts." I admitted wearily. "I'm tired and I'm hungry and... I'm tired." I wasn't about to say, 'And all I want to do is cry.'

"Let's eat something," Hudson said, lying beside me. "Maybe we'll feel better or at the least, we might have a little more energy to continue."

"Ugh, that means I'll have to get up," I whined. I was so reluctant to move that the idea of sitting up felt like a gargantuan task.

Hudson gently lifted me into a sitting position, his strong hands supporting my back as my arms dangled limply. While he rummaged through his pack for some energy bars, the drone returned, buzzing by us in the still air. We exchanged puzzled glances, wondering what it found.

Hudson set the bars beside me and began to do everything with the utmost care that touched my heart. He prepared the food, opened a bottle of water, and even held it for me to take sips. We discussed the odd reappearance of the drone, contemplating whether the operator was close enough to see us despite the drone's distance limit. Uncertainty hung in the air as we waited for a sign of what lay ahead.

We sat there after our meal was finished. I mustered the strength to give my profound gratitude to Hudson for everything he had done. "I promise you that I'll return the favor later, but I'm not just playing at being exhausted. My arms do **not** want to move."

Hudson's response was both comforting and affectionate. He pulled me close, and even though my arms hung limply at my sides, he pressed his lips to mine in a gentle kiss. I wanted to wrap my arms around him and return the kiss like I meant it, but I couldn't.

The high-pitched whine of the drone drew closer, interrupting us. It delivered a message, rose back up, and waited. Hudson picked it up and read it aloud.

> "While you rest, the time draws near,
> Endure today, let's be clear.
> Two miles hence, the crossing waits,
> Continue your journey, to your fates."

Hudson spoke to the drone operator. "We need some more rest. The gold is way heavier than you can imagine, and we're both exhausted." — I nodded in agreement. — "We need a break."

I'd reached my limit for physical endurance for the day, and I was certain that Hudson wasn't far behind me.

The drone buzzed away, only to return moments later with a note. My heart raced as Hudson unfolded it to reveal just two urgent words.

> "GO NOW!!!!!!!!"

# Chapter Seventeen

### Hudson

Taking Sarah's suggestion, we decided to move the gold bars a few at a time. It was a slower process, but it became apparent that neither of us could continue under the crushing weight of our initial loads. Sarah carried a single bar, and I took two, carrying them with our hands.

We began the painstaking journey towards the crossing point, each step feeling like an enormous effort. After what felt like a quarter of the way, we set the bars down, exchanging weary glances. There was no other option but to go back and repeat the process, again and again, until all the gold bars, the chest, and our packs were at the new location.

The cycle of carrying, resting, and returning continued relentlessly, our bodies pushed to their limits. Time seemed to blur as we repeated this grueling task, inching ever closer to our destination, with the drone flying over us occasionally, watching our progress.

As we finally had gotten everything to the crossing point, the sun was beginning its descent, casting long shadows across the rugged terrain. The weight of our ordeal pressed upon us, and we realized that we could not continue in the fading light. Our exhaustion was undeniable, and we needed to rest before attempting the final crossing.

With a shared understanding, Sarah and I decided to make camp for the night. The drone operator could go to hell for all I cared. We would need all the strength, and daylight, we could muster for the demanding task that lay ahead. I set up the tent and secured our supplies.

As we crawled into the tent, exhaustion pressed down on us like a ten-ton blanket. I needed to apologize for the situation we were in. My voice was filled with regret and exhaustion as I began, "Sarah, I'm sorry for this. I can't help but feel like this whole mess is my fault."

Sarah turned to me, her eyes reflecting both weariness and determination. "Hudson," she said softly but firmly, "this is not your fault. Remember that the first note was left on my doorstep. We're in this together, and I wouldn't want to be on this journey with anyone else. Yeah, it's been... incredibly hard, and it's not even close to being fun, but we can do this. We can and we will finish and then we'll find whoever it is who's doing this to us and make them pay," she said in a drowsy voice.

I drew her near me, holding her in my arms. Within minutes, the gentle cadence of her breathing reached my ears, and a soft smile crossed my lips. I hoped she would be in my life for a long, long time. Closing my eyes, I sighed contentedly and drifted to sleep alongside her.

I was jolted awake by the intrusive buzzing of the drone, my heart pounding in my chest as I realized Sarah was nowhere to be seen. Panic gripped me as the drone delivered its message, demanding we drop the gold and chest at the location, NOW! I guessed the rhymer got tired of making up rhymes.

As the drone departed, relief washed over me when Sarah emerged from the woods, carrying a small bag and looking considerably better than the previous evening. She explained that she needed to "take care of business." The scent of her toothpaste hung in the air.

I nodded, muttering something about needing to do the same, and hurried away. Upon my return, I found Sarah had taken down the tent and packed everything, ready to go. We exchanged dejected glances but knew we were nearing the end of this taxing journey.

We knew it would take longer, but we decided to take the bars a few at a time again. It was much easier and the thought of Sarah experiencing that much pain and exhaustion was too much for me.

Our first trip involved Sarah taking the chest and me taking two bars. After sleeping we had more energy to take them further and the entire process took less time to go further than it did yesterday.

Once we'd brought the last bar of gold and placed it in the chest where we thought it was supposed to be left, we continued on, back to the RV park. Conversation between us was non-existent but within an hour we were there. After a little more than ten hours of nearly constant walking, carrying more weight than we should have, we were both drained, mentally, physically, and emotionally.

Sarah headed for the shower in her cabin, and I ordered a pepperoni pizza, half with jalapenos. A hot meal after too many days of strenuous effort was exactly what we needed and more than anything, I hoped it would lift our spirits.

After I ordered, I headed for the shower in my RV. The warm water soothed my tired body and washed away the sweat and grime that clung to me over the past few days. I felt human again, still tired but human.

I sat on the porch of Sarah's cabin, gazing out at the tranquil surroundings, waiting for the pizza delivery. She joined me and the crisp, clean scent of perfume and soap filled the air. I inhaled deeply. It was a fragrance I found incredibly appealing. My thoughts wandered to the two of us, to where our relationship might be heading. We had been through so much already.

Once the pizza had been delivered, we sat at the table in Sarah's cabin and dug into the slices, savoring each bite as we discussed the first day at her new job tomorrow. It was the most normal thing we'd done in what seemed like forever.

After our meal, we conducted a thorough search of my RV and her cabin for any more bugs. We combed through every corner, every nook and cranny, but to our surprise, we found nothing. Even the one under the kitchen table had vanished.

• ♥ • ♥ • ♥ • ♥ • ♥ •

After everything Sarah and I'd been through in the past few days, I was bored just sitting around by myself. I wanted to call her, but I figured it might not be a good idea to disturb her at work.

I received a text from Sarah, and as I read her message, my brow furrowed with concern. She explained that there had been a mix-up with ranger housing, leaving her without a place to stay for another week. She asked if she could extend her stay in the cabin for that additional week.

I checked to find out if there were any vacancies, but they were all rented out. In my response, I explained that the cabins were fully booked, but I offered her an alternative. She could stay in my RV if she was comfortable with it. I assured her that there was a second bed, so she wouldn't have to share with me if she preferred not to.

Dinner time arrived, and I heard a knock on the door of my RV. I opened it to find Sarah standing there, looking grateful but also a bit apologetic.

"Thank you so much for letting me stay here, Hudson," she began, her voice filled with appreciation. "I know this is an inconvenience, and I'll make sure to find another place as soon as possible."

I looked at her, feeling a sense of warmth. "Sarah, it's really not a problem at all," I replied, a reassuring smile on my face. "If you're not comfortable staying here, I understand. But honestly, I have no issue with you being here as long as you'd like. You're more than welcome."

She seemed pleasantly surprised by my response. "Are you sure? I don't want to impose."

I nodded. "I'm sure. Consider it your home away from home for as long as you need it."

Sarah flashed a shy but appreciative smile. "Thank you, Hudson. I really appreciate your kindness," she said sincerely. "As a thank you, I'd like to treat you to dinner tonight. On my way here, I saw a Mexican food restaurant, and I've been craving it ever since I saw the place."

I wanted to spend more time with her, but I didn't want to spend any time in a vehicle. "I appreciate the offer, Sarah," I replied, "but I've been slow-cooking barbecue beef all day. How about we enjoy a quiet dinner here instead? I promise you, it's delicious."

"You mean... like those delicious barbeque sandwiches I've already eaten?" Her eyes sparkled.

"Exactly like that," I replied with a grin.

Sarah and I sat under the awning of my RV, the evening sun casting a warm glow over the campground and tops of the trees. The conversation flowed easily between us, and with each passing moment, I found myself drawn deeper into her world. Her laughter was infectious, and the way her eyes lit up when she spoke about her work as a ranger was captivating.

As we chatted about our interests, our dreams, and our favorite camping spots, I could feel myself becoming more and more attached to her. It was more than just the shared trials we'd been through; it was a genuine bond that was forming.

Sarah leaned back in her chair, gazing up at the darkening sky. "You know," she began, her voice soft, "I've always loved stargazing. There's something awe-inspiring about the night sky."

I nodded in agreement, my gaze shifting to the first twinkling stars. "I feel the same way. It's like a reminder of how vast and beautiful the universe is."

Sarah turned her attention back to me, her eyes searching mine. "Hudson, I want to thank you again for everything — for the treasure hunt, no matter how... forced and uncomfortable it was, for letting me stay here, and for being so kind."

I reached out and placed a hand on her arm, feeling the warmth of her skin beneath my touch. "Sarah, it's been my pleasure. I'm glad you're here, and I wouldn't have wanted to go on that... "adventure" with anyone else."

A comfortable silence settled between us as we watched the stars emerge one by one. Her smile was soft and genuine, and I knew that I wanted her in my life even more. It could be the beginning of something special if she wanted me in hers too.

"Hudson..." Sarah began softly. "Have you figured out who could be behind the rhymes? I mean... it would almost have to be someone who knows that you own the property. Nobody else would have cared so much about the place burning down... probably. Maybe it's someone local? Ugh, I'd love to just sit here and soak up the scenery with you, but I can't stand unfinished things."

I sighed, my gaze drifting to the stars above as I contemplated her question. "No, I wish I knew. I tried to do some research on the coins. I thought if there was a theft of them and the bars, there'd be a record somewhere but no luck."

I turned and faced her. "Are you planning on…" How could I ask what I really wanted to know? And why was it this hard? I'm a grown man and normally I'd just ask, but with Sarah it was different. She mattered. She mattered a lot to me, and I didn't want to push too much.

She looked down from the starry sky and faced me. "Am I planning on what?"

"Did you want me to make up the second bed?" Even I let myself down with that.

"Oh," she sounded disheartened. "If… you want to, it's okay with me. I thought… My mistake." She turned her gaze away and slowly rubbed her arms.

"No, no, no!" I needed to clarify myself and fast. "I mean, I didn't want to assume. I just… No, I don't want to. I want you to sleep in my bed." God! I sounded like such an idiot. "We don't have to do anything you don't want to. I promise. I just want to sleep with you in my arms again."

"Oh, I see," she still sounded disappointed.

I was a little slow, but realization soon dawned, and I stood and pulled her into my arms.

# Chapter Eighteen

Sarah

Hudson pulled me up and softly placed a kiss on my lips. I wanted him so much. He gently cradled the back of my head. His kisses were tender, but when he reached down past my waist, they became more. More passionate. More heated. And when his tongue entered my mouth, I was his.

He picked me up and I wrapped my legs around his hips. Our kisses didn't stop as he made his way into his bedroom. His scent excited me like no other. The combination of his cologne and the crisp, clean air was a healing elixir for my soul.

My heart was racing so fast, and my breathing became labored as we continued. Just from kissing, I was so close, it scared me. No man had ever brought me so close with so little. When it happened, I moaned and squeezed my legs together so forcefully, there was no way he didn't know what was happening to me. I was so embarrassed but the grin on his face was beautiful.

He lifted my chin with the side of his thumb, and I could feel the smile on his lips as he kissed me again. Slowly laying me on the bed, he crawled over me and trailed kisses to my ear.

"This should be fun," his baritone voice hummed as he lightly bit my earlobe.

I ran my fingernails through his hair, gently scraping his scalp, as he kissed his way down my neck. Slowly, he began raising my shirt up, caressing my skin the entire way up. He moved down to kiss my abdomen...

Loud and rapid knocking on the door interrupted our fun. Hudson groaned in frustration and his forehead softly hit my ribs.

"Go away," he muttered with exasperation. "Just go away."

"Hudson, it's Brice. I need to talk with you. Open up! It's important!" The voice on the other side of the door sounded desperate.

He looked up at me. The frustration and sadness in his eyes were disheartening but understandable. It seemed like the universe was conspiring to keep our private moments all too short and unfulfilled. He lightly kissed my stomach and stood up.

I looked at his pants. "Uh... you might want to sit down when you speak with whoever that is."

Hudson glanced down and groaned even louder, shaking his head in disbelief. "Stay here. I'll be back as soon as possible." With that, he headed to the door, leaving me on the bed.

From the bedroom, I listened to the conversation unfolding in the kitchen area. Hudson's voice was calm as he invited Brice inside. I couldn't see them, but their voices carried through the thin walls of the RV.

Brice's voice held an extreme amount of urgency as he explained the situation. His girlfriend and her two friends were overdue from a three-day camping and hiking trip, and he was growing increasingly alarmed. Hudson remained silent as Brice detailed their intended route, camping spots, and pick-up location.

As they discussed the hiking plans, my heart sank, realizing the gravity of the situation. Brice's desperation was unmistakable, and he pleaded with Hudson to help him now. However, Hudson told him that searching in the dark was a recipe for disaster.

I could hear Hudson reassuring Brice that Kim, his girlfriend, knew to hunker down for the night. It was clear that Brice was out of his mind with worry for his girlfriend. And as soon as Brice left, I headed for the bathroom. We would need sleep, not fun.

The next morning arrived far too early, but Hudson and I were already up and about. He was determined to begin his search for Brice's girlfriend and her friends, while I reluctantly prepared to head to work.

As I arrived at the ranger station, a sense of unease settled within me. It was evident that something was amiss as several rangers were gathered for an impromptu meeting. Benjamin, the park manager, stood at the front, his face etched with concern.

He wasted no time in addressing the situation at hand. The lost women were what he told us about. He asked for volunteers to join the search, and without hesitation, every ranger in the room raised their hand.

We were instructed to begin where the women had started their trip and call out their names — Kim, Diana, Courtney — in hopes of reaching their ears. The forest held its breath, and as we advanced further, groups of rangers branched off in different directions to explore alternative trails. A sense of urgency filled us. We knew that if any of them were injured, finding them quickly could mean the difference between finding them alive or not.

The longer we walked, the more I was pulled toward a distant mountain. Several rangers tried pairing up with me to search down trails, but I kept heading to that mountain. Benjamin showed up in one of the park's Gators, asking if we'd found anything.

"I think I saw smoke about halfway up that mountain over there," I stated cautiously, pointing in that direction. "It didn't last long, but I think I saw it. I'd like to check there." I prayed that my little lie wouldn't be discovered, but I needed to go in that direction.

"Hop in, Sarah, let's see what we can find," Benjamin said with a hint of astonishment.

The Gator bounced along the uneven trails at a speed I wasn't comfortable with. I reached over and touched his arm. "Could you slow down a bit? You never know what's around the next corner."

The Gator slowed down and I closed my eyes, feeling safer. When Benjamin slammed on the brake, it came to a screeching halt. I was thrown forward, the seatbelt cutting into my body as I braced myself with my hands against the inside of the little vehicle, grunting from the sharp pain.

"Did you know?" Benjamin asked, his eyes wide.

"We need to move it," I stated as I hopped out and headed to the fallen tree. It was much too big for the two of us to move it with sheer strength. The whirring noise of the winch on the front of the ATV spooling out the length of cable, reached my ears. I jumped over the tree and grabbed the end of the cable, throwing it under the trunk.

Benjamin hooked the cable to itself and trotted back to the ATV. He slowly backed up and began spooling in the winch at the same time. It strained with every inch and dirt flew from beneath the tires, but Benjamin kept at it as I pushed the tree itself. Finally, the tree began to move slowly. It seemed to take forever, but eventually, there was enough room for the Gator to pass.

I was sweating and my hands felt raw when I got back in the Gator. We continued on, but I could feel Benjamin looking at me. When I looked at him, he looked back at the trail.

"David told me you could do that, but I didn't believe him," he spoke loudly enough to be heard over the engine.

"I'd appreciate it if you would keep that to yourself. I saw smoke! If anybody asks, I saw smoke."

"Smoke it is," he said as he faced forward.

Once we reached the end of the trail, we started walking. The hike uphill was difficult. The sheer number of trees slowed our progress but eventually, we moved past the tree line, and they thinned out. While we didn't have as many trees to deal with, the incline continued to slow our movement.

As Benjamin and I trekked uphill, the strain became evident in our labored breaths. Our pace slowed, demanding frequent, short breaks. During one of our breaks, as I gasped for air, a faint but unmistakable sound reached my ears — the chilling scream of a woman. My heart raced, and I exchanged an alarmed glance with Benjamin.

We began our ascent again with renewed determination, but the farther we went up and the thinner the air got, I couldn't continue moving at any pace other than a slow one. My nerves were on edge, but I pushed myself to keep moving. My legs ached, my chest hurt, and I sucked in greedy breaths of air. Benjamin wasn't doing much better, and we had to stop again.

The next thing we heard, chilled me to the bone; a piercing scream too loud to be coming from a woman. Benjamin and I looked at each other, eyes wide.

"Mountain... lion!" Benjamin said between labored breaths.

The next sounds were unmistakable — the women's screams. Three distinct voices almost simultaneously filled the air. We pushed through the pain and moved faster.

As Benjamin and I closed in on the source of the screams, our breaths came fast and heavy, the adrenaline pumping through our veins. Then I saw it — a mountain lion, the largest cat I had ever seen up close. My heart raced, and I could feel my body tense up.

"Gun!" Benjamin shouted and fired a shot into the air, away from us. The deafening sound echoed in the wilderness, and the cat flinched and spun around, facing us. He fired two more times into the sky, each shot sending loud, powerful vibrations through the air.

The mountain lion hissed at us, its yellow eyes fixed on ours, but it turned and ran off. Relief washed over me as the majestic predator disappeared behind jagged rocks, continuing up the mountain and away from us.

The women's frantic calls reached our ears, asking if it was gone.

"It's gone," I reassured them as they squeezed out of a thin crevasse, their faces marked with fear and exhaustion. They ran toward Benjamin and me, their desperate voices echoing in the wilderness.

The descent down the mountain was less demanding, but my breath still came in ragged gasps, and my legs wanted to give out on me. All I wanted to do was lie down, rest, and breathe normally again.

As we approached the base of the mountain, the distant rumble of approaching ATVs reached our ears. Knowing that ATVs don't have unlimited seating, I felt a surge of relief wash over me, realizing that I wouldn't have to walk back on foot. I was certain I wouldn't have made it.

As we neared the Gator, four ATVs suddenly appeared on the scene. Each woman from the lost group climbed onto a different ATV, and together, we began our journey back toward the park entrance. I could sense the relief in the air, and the group that appeared was filled with smiling faces.

As we arrived at the rendezvous point, cheers and smiles welcomed us, especially from Brice. Someone had clearly radioed ahead that we'd found the missing women. The joy was evident as Brice and Kim embraced tightly, and Brice showered Kim's face with kisses. It was a heartwarming reunion, and I sighed in relief, grateful that the women were safe and sound.

As the group gathered around, people began to question Benjamin and me about how we had managed to find the missing women so quickly. I could feel the curious eyes on us, and I looked at Benjamin with a pleading expression, hoping he would handle this situation.

Benjamin took a moment, then replied with a calm and convincing tone, "We thought we saw smoke." It was a simple and believable explanation that seemed to satisfy the inquisitive crowd, and they nodded in understanding.

I stood there, relieved that the situation had been diffused with Benjamin's explanation. I felt a presence behind me, but before I could react, Hudson's voice whispered into my ear, "Smoke, huh?" The unexpected comment made me jump, and I turned to face him.

I nearly lost my balance, but I smiled as I playfully swatted his arm. "Yes, smoke!"

# Chapter Nineteen

### Hudson

I sat down next to Sarah at the picnic table, noticing the exhaustion in her eyes and the weariness in her posture. She let out a tired sigh, and I could tell she was hurting.

"My legs are killing me," she groaned, rubbing her thighs as if that might somehow alleviate the pain. "My arms aren't much better either."

I looked at her sympathetically and said, "You know, it's getting late, and you should be done with work by now. How about I drive you back to my place? I'll take you to work in the morning. Plus, maybe we can pick up where we left off last night," I said with a grin.

Sarah blinked at me, her expression held disbelief and amusement. "You're crazy," she said, but there was a playful glint in her eyes that told me she might just be considering it.

As I drove back to my place, Sarah nodded off in the passenger seat. Nearing my RV, rhythmic breathing reached my ears. I didn't want to wake her, but not only would her legs hurt in the morning, but so would her neck. I shut the engine off and walked around to get her out of the truck.

I thought she would wake up when I unbuckled the seatbelt, but I was wrong. Even the truck door shutting didn't wake her after I picked her up to carry her inside. Laying her on the bed, she rolled onto her side and didn't move. So much for picking up where we left off.

After removing her shoes and socks I wrestled with the idea of removing her clothes. She'd probably be more comfortable, but it would probably be a bad idea... for me anyway. Even if she didn't mind, I might.

The morning sun filtered through the window blinds, and I could smell the rich and inviting aroma of coffee wafting through the air, awakening my senses and promising a new day full of possibilities. I padded into the kitchen area just as Sarah finished making a second cup.

"Good morning!" she said with a cheerful smile. She was wearing a clean ranger's uniform, ready to go. "I'm just curious, how did I get here? The last thing I remember was sitting at a picnic table."

I gratefully accepted the hot coffee, took a sip, and sighed. It was perfect. "I brought you here." Taking another sip, I closed my eyes, savoring the roasted beans, with a hint of chocolate, and a touch of caramel sweetness.

"I kind of figured that, but... please don't tell me you carried me from the picnic bench." Her cheeks flushed pink.

"Nope, you walked there all on your own. You must have been way more tired than I thought if you don't remember."

"In my defense, I'm not used to the altitude here yet. And that mountain... it just about did me in. East Texas is kind of flat you know."

Setting the cup on the table, I wrapped my arms around her, breathing in her freshly showered scent, mixed with the soft fragrance of summer flowers. She smelled wonderful.

Sarah's phone rang and she pulled away slightly to answer it, her expression gradually shifted from contented to worried. The lines on her forehead deepened as she listened, and her responses became shorter. "Uh huh... I see... Okay... I understand... I guess it can't be helped..."

She sat heavily on the chair, her head cradled in her hands, tears falling onto the table. My heart clenched at the sight of her anguish. Swiftly, I grabbed a tissue and handed it to her. She wiped her face, her eyes red and weary. When she finally spoke, her voice wavered with emotion.

"It's all gone, Hudson," she said, her words heavy with disappointment. "My plan to save on rent is out the window. It feels like everything is falling apart. I thought with the raise I got for transferring here, I could pay off my college loans so much faster and start saving, but now... I don't even know if I can afford rent here."

I sat down beside her, reaching out to gently touch her hand. "Sarah, it's not the end of the world," I said softly, trying to offer some comfort. "Sometimes life throws curveballs, and we have to adjust our plans. You're not alone in this. I'll help you find a way through it."

She looked at me, her eyes filled with pain and distress. "But where will I live? I never even researched this area. I was supposed to have a place to stay already."

I took a deep breath, my mind racing with possibilities. "Sarah, you don't have to face this alone. I'll help you find a place. But, if you're comfortable with it, you could... you could live with me. I have that other room or... you could just use it for your clothes. Or I could."

The words hung in the air between us, thick with unspoken implications. Sarah stared at me, her expression held surprise and something I couldn't quite place. For a moment, the weight of her worries seemed to lighten, and I hoped she could see the sincerity in my eyes and that I was here for her.

Sarah looked at me, her eyes searching for reassurance. "Are you really sure about this, Hudson?" she asked cautiously.

I nodded, trying to convey my conviction. "Absolutely. I want you to be okay. I care about you, and I want to help you through this."

"What about rent? How much will you charge me for rent?" she inquired in a troubled voice.

"I could charge you whatever ranger housing costs would have been," I replied. "Or you could just live here and help pay for electricity and food," I added quickly.

Sarah hesitated, still skeptical. "I don't think you understand. Ranger housing is so much cheaper than any rental pretty much anywhere else in the U.S. And a month there costs less than a week here in the smallest cabin you've got."

I sighed, understanding her concern. "Would it make it better if I told you this RV is completely paid for? Besides, you're not just anyone. You're important to me. If you would prefer, I can help you look for a place, but in the meantime, I just want you to know that you have a place to stay, no matter what."

Sarah leaned into me, her arms wrapping around my shoulders. Gently, I pulled her onto my lap, holding her close as her sobs trembled through her. "It's going to be okay," I said softly, slowly rubbing her back.

"Don't worry about the housing right now. We'll figure it out," I reassured her, feeling her body tense slightly against mine. "You still have to get ready for work, though. Maybe a bit of routine will help, even if just for a little while."

She pulled back slightly, her red-rimmed eyes piercing my soul. "I forgot to tell you. While I was on the phone with Benjamin," she started, her voice shaky, "he gave me the day off to find a new place to live. It's a good thing, because my thighs are killing me, and walking is so, so, so painful. Of course, sitting is too."

I chuckled softly, cupping her cheek with my hand. "Then it's a good thing you're not working today. We'll figure out your living situation, and I've got an idea about what to do about your legs too." I grinned mischievously.

She looked at my lips, back up at my eyes, and squinted at me. "What idea?"

"If I had a tub, I'd have you soak in a warm tub with Epsom salt, but since I don't, you get a full body massage. I'll even play some relaxing music for you. And… make some warm Epsom salt compresses too."

"You know, from that grin you gave me, I wasn't expecting that." She looked a little puzzled.

"I know. But! Once your better…" I waggled my eyebrows.

She laughed. "So… you know how to give a massage. Are you any good?"

"Believe it or not, I thought it would be fun to learn so I went to a school for it," I stated authoritatively. "Why don't we spend the day exploring the town? There are some local places I'd love to show you, and maybe we can find a cafe to relax in. What do you think?

Besides, I need to get the oils for your massage." I suggested with a warm smile, genuinely excited about the prospect of spending the day together.

"I'm going to have to walk, aren't I?" Her eyes opened wide.

I had to laugh, she looked so cute when she was feeling sorry for herself. "Don't worry. I'll park close. If you need me to, I'll carry you." I winked at her.

Sarah smiled widely. "I'm going to hold you to that!"

We spent the day leisurely walking around the small town of Custer. Window shopping and walking through shops Sarah found interesting. Not once did she complain about being in pain, but I could tell that she was. Her strides were short, and her pace was half of normal.

Entering a quaint café, Sarah sat at a table closest to the entrance and I went to order. As I approached the counter, the aroma of freshly brewed coffee enveloped me. I decided on a rich, dark roast for myself and a soothing chamomile tea for Sarah. The barista, a friendly woman with a welcoming smile, prepared our drinks quickly. While waiting, I noticed a display of freshly baked pastries, and I couldn't resist grabbing a couple of croissants to share.

Carrying our drinks and pastries back to the table, I set them down, and we both sighed in contentment as the warm beverages offered a comforting contrast to the crisp morning air outside. "I hope you like chamomile tea," I said, passing Sarah her cup. "And these croissants looked too delicious to pass up."

As we sipped our drinks and indulged in the buttery croissants, we chatted about everything and nothing, savoring the simple joy of each other's company. The cozy ambiance of the café, coupled with our easy conversation, made it a perfect start to the day.

"This," — she said holding up the last bite of her croissant, — "is delicious." Popping it into her mouth, she moaned with satisfaction. "And this tea... uhm. I've never had chamomile tea before. It's uh... not my favorite. I hate to ask but would you please get me something different? Water is fine."

"Not a problem. I guess I should have asked." I felt bad about my poor choice, but I would make it up to her later. Bringing her a bottle of water, I told her to wait here; that I'd be back as soon as possible. She looked at me gratefully as she slumped over and rubbed her thighs. Leaving her at the table, I left the café to get what I needed for her massage.

I returned to the café after completing my purchase. Carrying a small white paper bag with handles and the name of the shop, colorfully displayed on the bag. Sarah was still slumped over, and she looked worn out.

"Whispering Crystals? What did you get?" she asked, one eyebrow raised.

"Something for your massage. I think you'll like it. Come on, let's go home and we'll see if we can do something to help with your arms and legs… and the rest of you." The grin on my face wouldn't go away.

"Sounds good. Give me a minute to stand and we can go." Her face was filled with pain as she rose.

"Here, let me help," I offered, slipping my arm around her waist to support her as she got up. Sarah winced slightly, but she managed a small smile. As we walked back to the truck, I was eager to help her feel better… and to be able to touch her body in so many places.

Once we arrived home, I led her to my bedroom, telling her I'd be right back, Sarah settled onto the bed, and I went to prepare for her massage. I returned with a plush bathrobe, told her to strip down to whatever level she felt most comfortable with, and left the room again.

# Chapter Twenty

### Sarah

Removing my pants was an interesting experience. I knew I'd be even more sore today, but this was ridiculous. I stripped down to just my panties and put the robe on. It smelled like Hudson. The woody and subtle sweetness of sandalwood only added to his natural appeal. Holding the collar over my nose, I inhaled deeply. His comforting and inviting scent filled my senses.

Hudson knocked on the door. "Are you ready?"

Opening the door and walking into the kitchen area, the scent of aromatic oils filled the small space, and soothing music played softly in the background. "I thought this might help you relax," he said, gesturing toward the setup.

Hudson had turned off the lights and flickering candles took their place. The kitchen table had been put away and a massage table stood in its place.

I smiled gratefully. "Thank you, Hudson. This is amazing. You even have a table for this. One question, do you have a step stool for me to use to climb up onto the table?"

He met my eyes, his were filled with warmth and affection as he lifted me and sat me on the table. "I just want you to feel at ease. Now, let's get started. I'll make sure your entire body gets all the care you deserve."

I slowly laid face down and Hudson removed the robe from my arms, covering me with a sheet. It sounded strange, even to me, but his scent being taken away from me was a little upsetting.

"I've put a "Do Not Disturb" sign on the door, so we should be good to go. I hope," he said with a hint of optimism in his voice.

As Hudson's skilled hands glided over my tired muscles, a wave of relief washed over me. The tension that had settled deep within my body seemed to melt away under his touch. Each stroke and knead felt purposeful, easing the knots in my muscles and releasing the stress I had carried for days.

His fingers moved with practiced confidence, finding the exact spots that ached the most. As he applied gentle pressure, I felt the tightness slowly giving way, replaced by a soothing sensation that seemed to seep into my very bones. It was as if he was unraveling the knots in my soul, not just my muscles.

The scent of the essential oils he used hung in the air, adding to the sensory experience. The room was filled with calming lavender, a slightly citrusy scent, a mild, sweet scent, a subtle herbal, and a slightly nutty fragrance embracing me in a cocoon of relaxation. With each movement of his hands, I could almost imagine the stress and exhaustion being carried away, leaving me lighter, both in body and spirit.

I closed my eyes, allowing myself to fully surrender to his healing touch. The rhythmic motion of his hands lulled me into a state of blissful tranquility. It was more than just a massage; it was a moment of pure indulgence, a precious break from the challenges I'd faced. I felt cared for, cherished even, and it made the experience all the more wonderful.

While he was working on my back, the tips of his fingers brushed across the sides of my breasts. Even if it was unintentional, it had been a while since a man had touched me like that and my mind began to wander. Small moans of pleasure escaped me as he worked.

Just as I thought he was about done, he told me to turn over so he could work on my front. I turned over, taking the sheet with me, and laid on my back. His hands began to work their magic on the fronts of my thighs. It hurt, but it also felt good, and I moaned louder.

Each time his hands got close to the inside top of my legs, I wished they'd go further. I was already aroused knowing who was touching my nearly naked body. A small smile crossed my lips and chill bumps covered my body. He was so strong, and I was putty in his hands.

"How are you feeling now? Any better?" he spoke softly.

"Wonderful," I said dreamily, my eyes still closed. "I don't want to get up."

"Good. Stay there and I'll be back in a few minutes," he said as he walked off.

The sound of rustling material reached my ears, and the next thing I knew, Hudson picked me up and carried me to his bed. He laid me on the sheet he'd spread over the covers and kissed me.

"You have no idea how difficult that massage was for me."

"I'm sorry. I didn't mean for you to—"

"You don't understand. It wasn't an inconvenience, I had to force myself to go slowly and not touch you in places I shouldn't."

"Why shouldn't you? I don't understand." Hudson's hand was on my belly in an instant and slowly heading up. "Oh… I see." I looked at his shirt. "I'm fairly certain you don't need that." He nearly ripped his shirt off. "And those." The bed bounced while he wrangled them off. "I've got to warn you though, my legs don't want to move."

"Don't worry about that. I'll take care of them for you," he said just before he kissed me again.

His kisses were soft and sweet, but the longer we kissed the more passionate they became. Our tongues met in a dance that sent shivers up and down my body. Slowly, so very slowly, he pulled the sheet down to my waist. Caressing my nipple with the pad of his thumb, he trailed kisses down.

I ran my fingers through his soft hair and scraped my fingernails along his scalp. He gently nipped the skin above my nipples with his teeth before he began sucking on it. Between his tongue's gentle swirling motion and his other hand working to remove my panties, I started squirming.

"Beautiful," he murmured in the dim light.

He could only lower them so far before he had to give the job more of his time and attention. I laid there, still reveling in the feelings of complete relaxation from the massage.

"So beautiful."

Standing at the end of the bed, he finished removing mine and then his own underwear. He was as ready as I felt. His wonderful massage techniques were at play again as he worked his way up my legs, massaging and making his way closer. I was lost in Hudson's eyes. As he leaned closer, a deafening explosion shattered the moment, and the RV shook violently as if caught in a fierce storm.

Hudson fell on top of me, covering my body and nearly crushing me with his weight. The world around us seemed to twist and turn, a disorienting dance of nauseating movement. The sharp sounds of breaking glass mingled with my screams, and the motion sent shockwaves of fear through my body. I couldn't catch my breath.

As abruptly as it had begun, the shaking ceased, leaving behind an eerie stillness. Hudson, still shielding me with his body, his protective embrace giving me a fragile sense of security.

"Are you okay?... Sarah! Are you okay?"

The fear in his voice prompted me to nod my head. "What... was that?" My voice trembled as I spoke in a whisper.

"An earthquake. They're usually not that strong. Did anything fall on you? Are you okay?" Hudson's voice slightly shook as he spoke.

"That was the scariest thing I've ever experienced," I said as he wiped tears from my face. "Are you okay? Please tell me you didn't get hurt." Even more tears fell at that thought.

We dressed and began surveying the aftermath. Miraculously, the windows were intact, but the once-orderly interior of the RV now lay in disarray. Cabinet doors hung open and dishes lay shattered on the floor, their demise a witness to the violent force of the tremor. The lit candles lay in puddles of wax. Hudson snuffed them out and surveyed the mess, looking frustrated.

"This mess can wait. I need to check on my guests," he said as he reached for a broom to clear the way to the door.

The scene outside was one of disbelief. Guests milled about or gathered in clusters, their faces etched with concern and the remnants of fear. Hudson and I made our way toward the people milling about. A wave of gratitude washed over us after we discovered that no one had been seriously injured.

The campground was a picture of contrasts. Most of the cabins stood undamaged by the earthquake. However, the RVs bore the brunt of the impact. Windows were shattered and two of the RVs had tipped over. The only saving grace for one of them was that the one lying completely on its side was unoccupied. The other one had been stopped from falling over completely by their own car, saving its occupants from a worse fate.

My phone rang and I clutched it tightly, the chaos of the earthquake slowly fading into the background as I answered Benjamin's call. His voice crackled with concern through the line.

"Are you all right, Sarah?" Benjamin's voice echoed in my ear.

I nodded. Realizing he couldn't see me, I quickly answered. "Yes, I'm fine."

"We're closing the park temporarily until engineers can assess the damage. Only repair crews will be working. You'll be paid, but it'll have to come from your vacation and personal days. Consider it an involuntary vacation until I call you back."

His words hung in the air, and a strange feeling of uncertainty settled in my chest. A forced break from work, yet the circumstances were far from relaxing. Trying to muster a smile, I replied, "Thanks, Benjamin. I'll be here, waiting for your call."

The evening was a whirlwind of activity, the aftermath of the earthquake demanding everyone's attention. Remarkably, the electricity in the area remained on, providing a welcoming trace of normalcy amidst the chaos. Aftershocks rumbled through the ground, reminders of the earlier violence, but they were gentler, more like nature's sighs of relief after the storm.

Hudson and I, along with the other campground guests, worked tirelessly, cleaning up cabins and aiding his visitors in salvaging what they could from their shaken RVs. The night wore on, and exhaustion settled deep into our bones. Despite our efforts, we weren't even halfway through the cleanup, but the lateness of the hour forced us to acknowledge our weariness.

After finishing as much as we could, we returned to Hudson's RV, sweat-soaked and dirt-streaked. We cleaned his RV and then took quick showers, the warm water washing away the remnants of the day's labor. Hudson's familiar scent filled my senses as he wrapped me in a tired, but loving embrace.

As the night settled around us, Hudson's tired voice broke the silence. "I can't thank you enough for helping with the cleanup," he said, gratitude running through his exhaustion. "I've never seen anything like this happen before."

I managed a small smile through my own yawns. "I'm just glad I could help," I replied, my voice heavy with weariness, mirroring his own.

We exchanged a few more words, the conversation peppered with yawns and stifled sighs. But the weight of the day finally caught up with us both. With a shared understanding, I suggested, "We should get some rest. There's still so much to do tomorrow."

Hudson nodded in agreement, his eyes already half-closed with fatigue. Climbing into bed, we found comfort in each other's arms, the faint scent of massage oils lulling us into a peaceful sleep.

# Chapter Twenty-One

Hudson

"Well... that was fun," Sarah said humorlessly. "Take pictures, clean up the mess. Take pictures, clean up the mess, and so on and so on and so on."

"Yeah, I'm sorry you have to deal with this. It's not even close to what I wanted to happen," I offered apologetically. "You want to take a shower first?"

"Have you ever thought about living in a regular house, you know, with a regular shower tub setup? And then—"

I sighed, trying to keep my composure. "I know the shower is small, but it's all I've got!" I couldn't keep the irritation out of my voice. I was giving her a place to live and all she could do was complain.

"Okay, I'm not going to hold the frustration against you. Too much has happened, but next time let me finish." While she spoke calmly, anger flashed in her eyes.

"I get it, okay? I'm doing my best here," I replied defensively. "This isn't easy for any of us, and I'm just trying to handle it the best way I can. But I need you to understand, too. I'm not trying to make things harder for you intentionally."

"Ugh!" She closed her eyes and sighed. "Stop. Just hang on a minute. I know you're not trying to make things harder for me. If you would have let me finish, you wouldn't be reacting like that... at all." She took a deep breath and opened her eyes. "I was going to say that we could take a shower together."

I leaned my elbow heavily on the table, covering my eyes as I sighed, realizing the depth of my mistake. My mind had jumped to the wrong conclusion. Sarah has been a huge help and I just jumped all over her for nothing.

"Sarah," I began, my voice softening as I met her eyes, "I would love to build a house, but the money just isn't available right now. There are too many repairs I need to make. I know I'll get a check from insurance, but I need to make repairs now."

Sarah gently reminded me, her words piercing through my clouded thoughts. "What about the rest of those little round gold things and the heavy gold bar things we hid in the cave?" She looked at me like I was clueless, but her beautiful smile was filled with understanding.

Her words hung in the air, and I blinked, stunned. How could I have forgotten about the gold? Well, I did know why but... It was as if a fog had lifted, and a glimmer of hope flickered in my mind. "You're right," I said, my voice brimming with newfound hope. "I can't believe I didn't think about that."

"Well, it has been a weird few weeks," she laughed softly. "Have you tried to figure out what they're worth? Even if the coins don't have any value other than the gold, the gold bars alone could solve all your money problems and then some."

"With everything that's been going on, my mind's been preoccupied with other things."

I've always kept my wealth hidden behind layers of a simple life; a carefully constructed facade designed to shield me from anyone trying to take advantage of the wealth I possessed. A few untruths to protect myself had been a given for me. Victoria had been a painful lesson, a reminder of how easily trust could be betrayed when money was involved. Since then, I'd grown wary, reluctant to let anyone get close enough to see the truth.

I preferred the quiet life, the rustic charm of the RV park, and the peacefulness of the forest. Money had never brought me true happiness. I loved having it, but it had attracted people like Victoria, people who saw me as a means to an end rather than as a person. So,

I kept my wealth a secret, avoiding discussions about finances and deflecting any inquiries about my background.

In the simplicity of my everyday life here, I found peace. My wealth was a closely held secret. It was a cautionary tale about the deceptive nature of appearances. I understood that not everyone was genuine. People often hid their true intentions behind friendly smiles. So, I opted for discretion, guarding my affluence as a shield against the world's unscrupulous eyes.

I wrestled with opposing thoughts in my mind, a battle between my desire to trust Sarah and my hesitations to reveal the truth. I wanted to tell her, to let her in, but the fear of betrayal and being used again held me back. The nagging doubts from my past made me cautious. History had taught me to tread carefully.

"Do you forgive me for jumping to the wrong conclusion? In my defense, it's been pretty damn rough for the past few days." I searched for empathy in her eyes.

Sarah smiled, her eyes soft with understanding. "Of course, but there's really nothing to forgive. If this was happening to me, I doubt I'd be handling this mess as well as you've been. And as long as we're good now, I'm going to take a shower. I'm exhausted, but I'm so glad we finished with what we could do. Who knows, maybe tomorrow we'll catch a break and have an easy day." Rising gracefully, she leaned in and pressed a soft kiss to my cheek, her touch lingering for a moment before she withdrew, leaving me to my own thoughts.

Before it was my turn to shower, I told Sarah to not fall asleep. I wanted to talk with her. I needed to find out if I could really trust her. I showered as quickly as I could and dried off. Like Sarah, I dressed in long pajama pants and a T-shirt.

She sat on the edge of the bed as I came out of the bathroom. "It's a good thing you're fast. Even sitting up, I'm starting to drift off," she said looking as tired as I felt.

Not even the shower woke me up as much as I hoped it would. We got under the covers, and I rolled onto my side, facing her. I placed my hand on her abdomen and found the hem of her shirt. Slipping under it, I caressed my way to her breast. Cupping it, I ran the pad of my thumb across her nipple. Tenderly, I continued. In the dim light, her eyes flew open, and she whimpered softly.

I moved slowly as I pulled her shirt up and over her head, reveling in the pure pleasure of seeing her bare breasts. They were firm, round, and felt perfect in my hand. Her eyes closed and she relaxed, sighing softly with a small smile on her lips.

Positioning myself over her, I leaned down and kissed her. Soft, lingering kisses led to more passionate ones. Our tongues swirled around each other as she pulled my shirt up. Removing one arm at a time, it hung around my neck. Stopping only long enough to remove the offending piece of clothing, she pulled my shirt off.

I pressed my chest against hers. The feeling of skin against skin excited me. Her firm body was a dream come true. No one would interrupt us this time. No one would stop us from completing this. I kissed her, holding her face tenderly.

When I went to remove her pants, I was never so grateful for our height difference. I didn't even have to stop kissing her, and she only had to bend her knees a little. I pressed myself against her, pulling her as close to me as possible. She did her best to get my pants off, but I had to help.

The excitement of what I wanted to do made it very difficult to go slowly. With as many times we've been interrupted, I was having a difficult time even wanting to go slowly.

"Don't... play around. I want... you in me," she said breathlessly between kisses. "We can... go slow... next... time."

Our underwear was gone within the next few seconds, and I felt the tip of my cock against her entrance. She was so wet, and I slipped in slowly. I knew I could go fast, but I doubted she would enjoy it very much, and I knew I wouldn't either.

I could feel the tight walls of her core gently squeezing me. God... it felt so good! I moaned deeply and shuddered. It was finally happening, and I reveled in the experience, taking every drop of pleasure out of this that I could.

I began sweating the longer I held myself back and took my time. I wanted to feel everything. Every sensation possible, I wanted it all. As I started to pull out, Sarah wrapped her legs around my hips, grimacing in pain. But when she locked her ankles together, she sighed with the most exquisite expression of bliss on her face that I'd ever seen.

She seemed to glow as I moved in and out, slowly, very slowly, building speed in tiny increments, and her smile widened. Her eyes were closed, and I could see she enjoyed having me in her. It was as if she had been without companionship for far too long, and she was going to imprint the experience so deeply into her mind that she would never forget.

Reaching up, she placed her hands on my shoulders and opened her eyes. Staring passionately into my eyes, she seemed to be seeing more than just my face. Extremely intense emotions welled up in me and it was almost too much to bear. I felt as if my body had been electrocuted, my nerves were on fire and tingled with more force than I'd felt before.

I sped up a little more and she opened her mouth, a moan of pleasure escaped, filling the room. I sped up a little more. A quick pulsing sensation hit me, and she tightened everything, and I mean everything. I didn't think her legs would squeeze as tightly as they did.

A look of pleasured pain crossed her face as she moaned loudly and arched her back. An absolute euphoric expression filled her entire being. It continued as I pumped faster and faster. I wasn't about to wait any longer.

Sarah may climax for longer than me, but I was going to give it my best to make it last. I was breathing harder, and it felt like my heart was beating faster than it had in a long time. I gasped for air as I felt myself getting closer. A guttural groan, louder than I expected came from me. I held onto the feeling and joined her. Pulses of pure pleasure radiated from me in waves of ecstasy. Locking my elbows, my entire body tensed, and exhaustion overcame me.

Sarah giggled. "That was... wow! Just... wow!" She covered her face with her hands. "Probably shouldn't be talking when my brain's not working right."

Resting on my elbow, I slowly pulled her hands away from her face. "You... can talk all you want." Brushing a strand of hair out of the way, I kissed her cheek. "Just wait until we can spend more time together and some bizarre tragedy isn't interrupting us."

She looked me in the eyes and placed her hand on my chest softly. "I'm looking forward to that. I was afraid someone would interrupt us again."

I chuckled. "Yeah, that same thought went through my mind too. Even if someone tried that, I wasn't about to stop and leave this time. They'd have to wait."

Well, so much for talking to Sarah about my financial situation. It's probably better anyway. I like her and I want to spend time with her, but I'm still not sure that my wealth won't change things and she turns out to be just like Victoria.

Sarah rolled to face me and placed her hand on my arm. Her eyes were closed, and her breathing sounded like she was asleep. I closed my eyes, my mind raced with what-ifs.

# Chapter Twenty-Two

### Sarah

I looked around at all the children in my group. "… And that's why we "Leave No Trace" when visiting the forest. Remember, whenever you explore the outdoors, the less we leave any evidence of us humans being around, the healthier the park will be and the healthier our planet will be. Every time you go outside, even if it's only in your own neighborhood… if you see any trash, pick it up and dispose of it properly. Thank you for coming to this beautiful park. Please enjoy the rest of your day here and come back soon."

After finishing my talk, I smiled at the group, acknowledging their appreciative nods. The children seemed engaged, their curious eyes reflecting the wonders of the natural world. As the group dispersed, some families headed for the nearby picnic area, while others ventured toward the hiking trails.

I settled beneath the comforting shade of an ancient tree, its massive roots providing a comfortable perch to take a break. The picnic area buzzed with families and laughter, the atmosphere relaxed and cheerful. As I unwrapped the other half of my sandwich from lunch, I overheard an intense conversation nearby, the voice strangely familiar.

My curiosity was piqued as I discreetly observed a woman a few yards away with her back to me, engrossed in a heated phone call. I'd seen her walking away from me too many times not to recognize her. It was Victoria, the very person who'd been involved with

Hudson, her voice sharp with annoyance. I eavesdropped as she vented her frustration on the phone.

"Where the hell have you been? I've been trying to reach you forever! You told me about the gold, but you don't seem to care if I found it!" Victoria's voice was full of anger. "Well, clearly it was more than just a legend because I found it. Gold bars and coins."

She huffed and groaned, clearly whoever she was talking to was irritating her to no end or that's just her default setting. "They're Capped Bust Gold Five-Dollar Half Eagle coins... Don't be an idiot, they're worth a lot! Melting them would be stupid! We're looking at nearly sixty thousand dollars for selling just one of them. Melting them wouldn't even get a thousand dollars..."

I listened more intently when she mentioned the five-dollar coins, straining to hear her better.

"There were four coins and three gold bars... No, they were too heavy," she said in an irritated tone. "I left the bars there. I took the coins with me, they're worth more than the bars... No! You have to go with me to get the bars. You need to carry them. I've already done most of the work after you left! It's your turn to do the heavy lifting. I hid them. I'm not an idiot! I'm not you!" she spat; her words dripped with disdain. Standing up, she grumbled to herself. "Are you kidding me? If you can hear me, I'll call you back. Stupid reception!"

I stayed where I was, hidden behind the tree. My mind raced with the implications of what I'd heard. Victoria's words left me stunned; my thoughts twisted in knots as I considered how to handle this unexpected revelation. The quiet picnic area suddenly felt too open, too unsafe. If she saw me here, it would be a real problem.

The only issue I had with what she said was the number of bars and coins didn't match what Hudson and I had taken with us to give to the rhymer. Either it wasn't what we found, or she had no intention of sharing all of it with her friend and planned on keeping the lion's share herself.

I needed to tell Hudson, and fast! And I needed to find someplace with good cell reception.

I tapped my foot impatiently as the phone rang. When the recording came on, I left a message. "Hudson, this is really, really important. I need to talk to you. Can you come to the park? Please, call me as soon as possible and let me know. I'm getting off in a couple of hours. If you don't call... Oh, dear God. I guess I'll see you at home."

Time crawled at a snail's pace as I waited for Hudson to call, or it was time for my shift to end. An hour later, he still hadn't called back. I had to give another talk, so I turned my phone off.

As the sun dipped low on the horizon, casting long shadows over the park, I wrapped up my final tour of the day. The laughter and chatter from people in the park slowly faded into the background as I made my way to my SUV.

I pulled into the RV park and spotted Hudson busy replacing broken windows. I slipped inside the RV, feeling a strange mix of restlessness and excitement. Pacing within the confined space, I waited for Hudson's return. My mind buzzed with thoughts of Victoria's phone conversation and what we could do to screw up her plans to retrieve the gold she'd basically stolen.

The sounds of power tools finally ceased, and I hoped it meant Hudson was done for the day. Hearing footsteps approaching, I opened the door to greet him. His tired smile eased some of the tension I was feeling. With an affectionate kiss, he told me he was going to take a shower.

Left alone, I busied myself by preparing a cup of coffee, the familiar hiss and gurgle of the Keurig machine drowned out the thoughts in my head. The aroma of freshly brewed coffee wafted through the RV, adding to my sense of relaxation.

Minutes later, Hudson emerged from the shower with a towel wrapped around his hips, the steam dissipating around him, leaving his skin warm and slightly flushed. As he wrapped me in a hug, I couldn't help but breathe in deeply, taking in the comforting scent of soap and clean skin. It was a scent that felt like home, like safety.

I popped a K-cup into the coffee machine to make a cup for him, my hands slightly shaky as I recounted the details of what I had overheard from Victoria. Hudson's brow furrowed in disbelief as he listened. With each word, I could sense his mind working, processing the information. I finished and met his gaze. His downcast expression, caused by the newest betrayal from Victoria, made my heart feel heavy and a physical pain radiated out in my chest.

Hudson exhaled heavily. "Oh God," he said, completely disheartened. "Are you sure you heard correctly? Are you positive it was Victoria? Of course, it was. I knew she wasn't a good person, but I never expected this," he said, barely above a whisper.

"I'm so sorry. I wish I hadn't... I'm..." I didn't know what to say. How could someone be so cruel to him, he's such a wonderful person.

"I'd bet almost anything that Victoria came here in the first place to get back with me so that she could get that gold sooner. And when that didn't work, she threatened to burn everything down. God! How could I have ever felt anything for that bitch!"

He started to get angry. Angrier than I'd ever seen him get before. The look on his face made my eyes widen and I took a step away from him. When he realized what I'd done, his expression changed, and he looked at me, his brows raised and eyes widened. He stood up and stepped toward me, reaching for me.

I shook as he pulled me to his chest and embraced me. I was surprised by his tenderness. He spoke softly. "Thank you for telling me. I apologize for letting my anger get the better of me. I promise you, none of it was because of you." He kissed the top of my head tenderly and rested his cheek there. Slowly rubbing my back, his calming touch eased my mind. I relaxed and wrapped my arms around his waist. Resting my ear against his heart, it slowed the longer he held me.

"If Victoria really did hide it, would you like for me to help you look for it? Maybe we can find it and get some more of your property back," I asked cautiously.

"Are you working tomorrow?" he said pulling away a little from me.

"No, but it might be better if we went tonight. I'd really hate it if she, and whoever she was talking with, came tomorrow morning and they got it instead of you. We can just grab our backpacks and some flashlights and go." I was willing to go at night only because Hudson would be with me, and I knew he would protect me. "Night might not be the best time but I'm sure Victoria won't waste any of it herself."

Hudson looked a little unsure about this, but after I kind of pushed him to do it, he agreed. He had such a strange... aura about him. It was difficult to describe, but it was almost as if he didn't trust me. Nevertheless, we left to see what we could find.

Compared to the last time, it didn't take us very long to get to where we left the chest, and we looked around for where it might be hidden. We spotted the trail through the grass at almost the same time and followed it. Clearly, Victoria had made a few trips to carry the gold bars and had worn down the path enough that it was still flatter than the rest of the grasses. It was fairly easy to find after that. We loaded the backpacks and carried the chest, taking it back to the RV.

The trip back was considerably quieter than I expected, but considering the weight we were carrying, maybe Hudson wanted to save his strength. I tried talking to him, but, if I was lucky, the most he said were one- or two-word answers. By the time we were halfway back, I'd given up speaking to him.

"Well, that was easier than I thought," I said humorously once we made it back to the RV, and I removed my backpack. "Any ideas about what to do about Victoria? And what do you think she'll do when she finds out the gold is gone?"

"I don't know," he said in a flat tone.

"Hudson? What's wrong? I thought you'd be happier than this. You've gotten some of your gold back." I was so confused by his demeanor. "You can get your campground fixed now and not have to worry about waiting for a check from the insurance company."

"I'm going to put this someplace safe." He was still wearing his backpack. Grabbing mine, he went to his room.

His monotone voice worried me, and I was so confused. This isn't how someone acts when they've gotten a windfall of any kind. Making a couple of cups of coffee, I waited in the kitchen area until he came back. After he'd been in his room for twenty minutes, I knocked on the door.

"Hudson? When you get done in there, I made some coffee for you." I tried to sound normal, but I wasn't sure if I succeeded. He didn't answer and I knocked again. "Hudson? Are you all right?" He still didn't answer, and I tried the door. It was locked.

I quietly grabbed the things of mine I could and left. Sitting in my SUV, I hoped he would come out and stop me, but he didn't. The tears wouldn't stop as I drove away and toward Custer to find a hotel room. I didn't know what I'd done but I wasn't about to stay there when every fiber of my being was screaming for me to leave. I could get my things tomorrow... I guess.

# Chapter Twenty-Three

### Hudson

Walking back to the RV felt like treading through the same thick fog from my past. Every step weighed on me, dragging my soul down into the muck and mire. Sarah kept trying to engage me in conversation, but her words barely reached me. I felt lost in the whirlwind of my thoughts.

Once inside the RV, Sarah tried to inject humor into the situation, her attempt at cheerfulness contrasted sharply with the heaviness in my heart. "Well, that was easier than I thought," she said, her tone laced with mock amusement, and she shrugged off her backpack. "Any ideas about what to do about Victoria? And what do you think she'll do when she finds out the gold is gone?"

"I don't know," I replied, my voice devoid of any emotion.

Sarah looked at me, confusion etched across her face. "Hudson? What's wrong? I thought you'd be happier than this. You've gotten some of your gold back. You can get your campground fixed now and not have to worry about waiting for a check from the insurance company."

Victoria had shattered my ability to trust. "I'm going to put this someplace safe," I said, my voice flat. Still wearing my backpack, I grabbed Sarah's and went to my room.

Behind the locked and closed door, I placed the gold in a hidden compartment, my fingers tracing over the cool metal. But the thrill I should have felt wasn't there. It had been replaced by a lingering dread. My past, filled with deceit and manipulation from Victoria, had cast an ugly, dark shadow over my present, clouding my judgment and leaving me with a bitter taste of distrust.

The fear of being deceived again weighed on me like a bank's cast iron safe, trapping me in a cycle of distrust and fear of being hurt again. As I sat on the edge of the bed, I couldn't escape the realization that my past was threatening to destroy a future that could be with Sarah... if she could be trusted.

A soft tap sounded on the door. "Hudson? When you get done in there, I made some coffee for you."

I wanted to respond, but the words wouldn't come out.

"Hudson? Are you all right?"

I wanted to tell her that it wasn't her, that she had done nothing wrong. But I was drowning in the sea of my own insecurities.

I heard the faint sound of the doorknob turning, but the door remained closed, locked against the world outside, against her. I sat there, paralyzed, caught between the weight of my thoughts and the reality of the situation. The distant sound of the RV door closing reached my ears, followed by the low growl of Sarah's SUV coming to life. It roared into existence, tearing away into the night.

I should have moved, should have leaped to my feet and chased after her. But I didn't. Anger surged within me, not at her, but at myself. Frustration and regret knotted in my chest, constricting like a vise. How had I let it come to this? How had I pushed away the one person who had shown me genuine kindness and cared for me after so long?

As the sound of the departing SUV faded into the distance, the weight that had held me down suddenly lifted. The realization hit me like a thunderclap — I hadn't stopped her from leaving. I'd let my fears and insecurities win. I slammed my fist into the mattress, the frustration burning through me.

I felt like a fool. I cursed under my breath; my jaw clenched with determination. I couldn't let this be the end. I couldn't let my past dictate my future. With newfound resolve, I sprang into action. I needed to find her and make things right, to prove that I wasn't the broken man my past suggested.

In the stillness of the night, I stormed out of the RV, my eyes fixed on the road ahead. Sarah was out there, driving away from me, but I refused to let her slip through my fingers. Whatever it took, I was going after her.

My truck roared to life, and I took off. The night air rushed in through the open window, sharp and cold, matching the urgency pulsing in my veins. Frustration gnawed at the edges of my mind. Where could she have gone? I knew she wasn't familiar with many places in town. She must have stuck to the places she knew, and the park's proximity meant Custer was her likely destination. Every streetlight flickered past like a fleeting hope, my eyes scanning the shadows for Sarah's SUV.

Custer wasn't a sprawling town, but in my desperation, every street felt like a labyrinth. I circled the parking lots of every hotel I came across, my eyes searching for her SUV among the rows of parked cars. The minutes stretched into eternity as I covered every inch of ground I could.

With a sinking feeling, I retraced my steps. My eyes never rested; my heart pounded in my chest. The night seemed endless, the world reduced to the beam of my headlights and the hope that I would find her.

And then, like a beacon in the darkness, I saw it — her SUV, parked in front of a store's parking lot. Relief flooded through me, mingled with a profound sense of urgency. I pulled in, cutting the engine as I watched her emerge from the store, a plastic bag in her hand.

She looked up just as I stepped out of the truck, her eyes widening in surprise, maybe even a hint of relief. For a moment, neither of us spoke, the weight of unspoken words hanging between us.

"Sarah!" I called, my voice rough with emotion. "Sarah, wait!" Each step I took toward her felt like a leap of faith. I had to make her understand, had to bridge the chasm that I had opened up between us. Whatever it took, I was determined to do it.

She trembled as I gently held her arms. Her eyes, once bright, were now red and swollen. She didn't say a word, but the silent sorrow in her eyes spoke volumes.

"Sarah," my voice softened, filled with regret, "I'm so sorry. I messed up back there, I shouldn't have shut you out. I should have told you the truth, about me and what happened with Victoria." I paused, searching for the right words, the ones that would mend the shattered trust she must be feeling. "I was afraid. Afraid of being used again, of someone else wanting me only for my money. But I see how wrong I was, and how much I hurt you."

I pulled her into a hug, holding her close as if to shield her from the pain, my words a whisper against her hair. "I can't promise you that everything will be perfect, but I can promise you honesty from now on. I care about you, Sarah, more than I've ever cared about anyone. I don't want to lose you because of my stupidity."

I met her gaze, my eyes sincere, pleading for understanding. "Please, follow me back to the RV. Give me a chance to explain. I want to make things right with you."

It took some convincing, some shared silences filled with unspoken apologies and promises from me, but eventually, she nodded, my grip on her arms softening. At that moment, a glimmer of guarded hope flickered in her eyes, a slender thread connecting us amid the damage I caused.

I settled into my seat at the table, my hands trembling slightly as I prepared the coffee, dropping a K-cup into the machine. The soft hum of the coffee maker filled the RV, creating a momentary distraction from the weight of the conversation I was about to start.

Sarah put the black plastic bag on the table. My thoughts raced as I searched for the right words to say. What I did, shattered the trust we'd built, and I knew I had to be honest, even if it made me feel uncomfortable.

I took a deep breath, trying to steady my voice. "Sarah," I began, my eyes meeting hers, "I need you to know something. I've been keeping a secret, and it's time you knew the truth."

I hesitated, the words catching in my throat. "I'm... wealthy. Like, really wealthy. I paid for this RV, the RV park, my truck, the land, all of it in cash. I pay cash for everything. I didn't need to sell any property or get loans. When Victoria found out about my wealth, she changed. She became demanding, always wanting more — more vacations, a new car, designer clothes. The list of her wants never ended. She wanted a lavish lifestyle, a mansion where she could indulge in her every whim."

I glanced away, trying to compose myself. "But I didn't want that. I wanted to build this RV park and live this life. I wanted something real, something I could build from the ground up. I thought she loved me for who I was, not for how much money I had. Eventually, I couldn't stand feeling used by her all the time. I couldn't take it anymore. That's one of the reasons why we broke up... and her probably cheating on me was another reason."

I looked back at Sarah, my eyes pleading for understanding. "When you pushed me to find the gold during the middle of the night, I thought... I thought you were after my money too. But after you left the RV... I don't know what to believe anymore. I need you to trust me, Sarah, and I want to trust you.

"Do you like chocolate?"

"Huh?" She had me confused with that question.

"Do you like chocolate?"

"Uh... Yeah. Why do ask?"

Sarah reached into the bag, took out a package of dark chocolate truffles, and opened it. She poured the contents onto the table and pointed to them. "Chocolate's supposed to make you feel better." She opened one and ate it, a small smile playing on her lips. I smiled and picked up a truffle. Popping it into my mouth, I savored its rich, creamy taste. In that simple exchange, I felt like maybe, just maybe, we were going to be okay.

For a little while longer, we sat at the table, the rich aroma of coffee lingering in the air as we indulged in the dark chocolate treats. Each bite was a small comfort that built upon the last one.

As the minutes passed, the weight on my shoulders seemed to ease, replaced by a sense of calm in her presence. Eventually, we finished our coffee and the last of the truffles. Wordlessly, we cleaned up, throwing away the wrappers and washing the cups.

When everything was in its place, we made our way to bed. The events of the day, the emotional rollercoaster we had both endured still hung in the air between us. I knew there was still more that needed to be done to fix things, but this was a good start.

Under the soft glow of the RV's interior lights, we settled into bed. "Can I hold you?" I whispered. Wordlessly, she scooted closer, her back to me. She smelled like the outdoors and summer flowers, and I breathed in deeply, relaxing even further. This was where I wanted to be and this is where I wanted her to be, in my arms.

With the quiet of the night and Sarah nestled in my arms, her presence was a soothing balm to the unrest inside me. Her unspoken forgiveness surrounded me, easing my mind a little more with each passing second.

The weight of my earlier mistakes and the fear of losing her began to lift. In the gentle rhythm of her breathing, I found comfort. It was a moment of silent understanding, where words were unnecessary, and the simple act of being together spoke volumes.

I held her a little tighter as if trying to convey my gratitude through the strength of my embrace. As I closed my eyes, I allowed myself to believe, if only for that moment, that we could navigate the challenges ahead together. Her forgiveness was a gift, and I vowed silently to cherish it, to cherish her, for as long as she would have me.

# Chapter Twenty-Four

### Sarah

I strolled around the park, my mind still sorting through the events of the previous night with Hudson. The uncomfortable cloak of our conversation clung to me like a thick, stubborn fog. As I chatted with guests, I noticed Victoria, the epitome of sophistication, with a man who seemed to be her complete opposite. He was wearing faded blue jeans with holes at the knees and a heavy metal band T-shirt, also with holes. His appearance was in stark contrast to Victoria's polished appearance. Intrigued, I edged closer, trying to overhear their conversation amidst the park's background noises.

Approaching Victoria, she glanced in my direction before returning to her conversation with the guy. I couldn't help but chuckle inwardly. It seemed that either she didn't recognize me or, more likely, my ranger uniform rendered me invisible in her eyes, or I was just too unimportant for her to notice. It was a strangely liberating feeling, knowing that I could observe without being noticed, at least for this moment.

I stood with my back turned to them and didn't hear everything the guy said. I only heard the last part of what he said. "... the gold and you really did hide it?"

Victoria's words dripped with condescension. "Yes. Unlike you dear brother, I'm not an idiot. I have Hudson wrapped around my little finger. He'll do whatever I want him to do."

Her confidence puzzled me. How could she be so sure she could do that?

The brother, clearly skeptical, questioned her motives. "What if he won't do whatever you want? I thought you two broke up."

Victoria sounded as smug as ever. "It's not like I can't bend his will to mine. I've done it before, and I can do it again."

Her response sent shivers down my spine, chilling me to the bone. Was she talking about basically forcing Hudson and me to get that gold for her? Or was it something else?

As they walked away, the feeling of unease nearly drowned me. Why were they even in the park? And what did she mean by "bending his will"? I had way too many questions and not enough answers.

Not long after they left, Victoria came back, heading for the parking lot, but the brother wasn't with her. Considering the brother's appearance, he could be living in the park, and he seems to have been doing it for a while.

I pulled out my phone and quickly sent a text to Hudson, asking him to come to the park, telling him it was important. I hit send, hoping there was enough reception to send it and that he'd receive the message soon. There was a knot of anxiety in my stomach. Apprehension and urgency filled me as I waited for his response.

Throughout the day, I kept my eyes peeled for any sign of the brother, but I didn't see him again. As the sun dipped closer to the horizon, Hudson arrived at the park with a concerned look in his eyes.

"Hudson," I began. I didn't want to pile more on him concerning Victoria, but he deserved and needed to know. "I saw Victoria today with a guy she called her 'dear brother.' Do you know if she has one?"

He shook his head, his expression showing uncertainty. "I've never heard her mention a brother, but who knows with her. Deceit and lying are practically her default modes."

I took a deep breath, unsure how he would take the information I needed to tell him. "She talked with the guy about hiding the gold and said something about bending your will to hers... that she's done it before and can do it again." I watched as Hudson's face shifted from curiosity to anger, his jaw tightening.

"Damn," he muttered, his tone filled with frustration. "I hate to say this, but she was always good about convincing me to do what she wanted. I was so gullible... but not anymore. Not where she's concerned anyway."

I shrugged, understanding the feeling of being manipulated and lied to. "I was shocked by what she said, but I thought you should know." Not wanting to add to the feelings Hudson was feeling last night, I added quietly, "I just wish I wasn't the one telling you."

Hudson tenderly touched my cheek and his gaze softened. "Don't say that. I appreciate you telling me. I just wish I knew what to do about this. Her mind is so warped."

I nodded, my mind racing with possibilities. "There's a chance that the brother is living in the park. Parks are huge and there are a lot of places, way off the beaten paths, that park guests just don't go into. He was pretty scruffy-looking. If he can be found, maybe you can get some answers. But... it's too dark to start looking. I have to work tomorrow, but maybe you can start looking for him."

Hudson wore a frustrated expression. "I have no idea what the guy looks like, and I have no clue where to even start looking. Ugh!" His frustration grew by the second. Taking a deep breath, he continued, "I'll start looking tomorrow, but is there any way you can help me?"

"I'll see what I can do," I said cautiously, slowly shaking my head. "I'll talk to Benjamin and see what I can figure out. In fact, I'll go right now. I think he's still here." I hoped he was, anyway.

· ♥ · ♥ · ♥ · ♥ · ♥ ·

I parked my SUV beside Hudson's truck, the early morning sun cast long shadows through the trees. Knowing that the people living illegally in national parks have a tendency to be on the criminal side, Benjamin had rearranged the schedule so a search could be made. He also warned me that, due to budget constraints, we only had one day to find the man. Dan, one of the law enforcement rangers, armed and ready, joined our little group.

The morning air was cool and crisp, carrying the scents of clean air and pine. The dense foliage surrounded us as we left the main path. The silence of the forest seemed to amplify our footsteps. As we moved forward in silence, I wondered about the brother. What had brought him here to hide in the national park? Was he dangerous, or was he just here because of the gold?

With every step, our eyes scanned the surroundings, looking for any traces of human presence. The park, usually a sanctuary, now felt edged with danger. I kept my senses sharp, aware of every rustle and movement around us.

Following what looked like an unusually wide animal trail, the hours passed, and the sun climbed higher in the sky. As we continued our search, I couldn't shake the feeling of being watched. The forest, usually serene and comforting, now felt alive with unseen threats. I exchanged a glance with Hudson, his expression mirroring my unease. Facing forward I whispered, "You feel it too?" I reached for his arm.

Hudson nodded in agreement. We continued but with every passing moment, it felt like we were getting closer. My steps slowed as the unmistakable feeling of imminent danger assaulted my senses. Dan, a few steps ahead of us slowed his pace as well until we all came to a stop, listening to the forest.

In the tense silence, Dan, Hudson, and I stood on high alert, our awareness heightened, sensing danger lurking nearby. The air crackled with tension, and I could practically feel the adrenaline pumping through my entire body.

A soft scratching sound sliced through the stillness, and before I could react, a man lunged out from behind a tree with astonishing speed. He tackled Dan, aiming to take the still-holstered gun. Hudson sprang into action, joining the skirmish, and the three of them wrestled fiercely on the forest floor.

Amidst the chaotic struggle, I found my opportunity to contribute. Swiftly, I repositioned myself and aimed a well-placed kick at the man's groin, not intending to cause serious harm but certainly wanting to get his attention. "Stop!" I warned in a firm voice. "Keep fighting, and the next thing you'll feel is crippling pain. Understand?" I hissed at the man as both Dan and Hudson looked back at me, grinning like Cheshire cats. My heart raced so fast; I thought it would beat out of my chest.

The man, still face down, nodded and didn't move. His wild, animal-like struggling stopped under the threat of pain, Dan wrangled the man's arms behind his back, and, using flex cuffs, he secured him. Dan and Hudson pulled him to his feet.

The man, whom I recognized as Victoria's brother, glared at me. Hudson quietly asked if he was Victoria's brother, and I gave him a subtle nod. We needed information from Victoria's brother, and it had to be done discreetly, without raising any suspicion from Dan, or anyone else.

As Dan read him his rights and started questioning the man, I subtly moved closer to Hudson, and whispered, "We need to talk with him... alone. Let me see what I can do."

I took a step forward, catching Dan's attention. "Dan, I've seen this guy before. I think he's been in the park for a while. He might have some mental health issues. He's been wandering around and... he might just need some help," I suggested, trying to sound convincing.

Hudson nodded subtly, playing along. "Yeah, I've seen him a few times too. Always seemed a bit lost," he added, reinforcing my story.

"Uh... yeah and what are you doing here in the first place? Benjamin said you were coming along, but I want to know why. You're not law enforcement." Dan gave Hudson a questioning look.

"I'm a volunteer with search and rescue. Considering the lack of a full law enforcement unit for this park, I volunteer to help when I can. And I wanted to make sure that Sarah would be okay."

Dan looked between us and grinned. "If she was my girlfriend, I'd want to protect her too. I can understand that. All right, but we still need to figure out what he's doing here. Let's get him back to the ranger station. I'll call for someone from social services to check on him."

That was a little embarrassing to hear, but I hoped it would be enough to make him stop questioning Hudson's presence.

"Maybe we could act like we're trying to help him," Hudson suggested. "If he really is Victoria's brother, he might be more than happy to help us. We could appeal to his vulnerabilities. With Victoria involved, I'd bet he knows she doesn't give a crap about him, and that he'll be used and thrown away when she's done with him."

Nodding in agreement, I added, "If we can make him see us as allies, he might be more willing to open up."

Hudson agreed, his eyes cutting toward Victoria's brother. "He might not even want to help her at all, and he's being manipulated into it. Maybe it happens so much that it's normal for him."

I was wracking my brain, trying to figure out a way to talk to Victoria's brother alone, when Dan stopped and held his hand up to his ear. After a few seconds, he turned around and looked at Hudson and me with concern in his eyes.

"A group of poachers were spotted not far from here," he said in a serious tone. "I need to handle this immediately. I need to leave him with you. Will you two be all right?"

We nodded, and Dan passed the man into Hudson's custody before rushing away.

# Chapter Twenty-Five

Sarah

As soon as Dan was out of earshot, I took a deep breath, steadying my nerves. It was time to start the conversation that could hopefully shed light on the situation. "What's your name?" I asked, my tone gentle.

"Why should I tell you? You were going to kick me in the nuts," he grumbled.

"Well... I don't know if you are or not, but I'm tired of calling you Victoria's brother." I figured honesty might be the best policy right now. His eyes grew wide at the mention of Victoria's name.

"You are her brother, aren't you?" His reaction said it all, but the wicked grin on his face confused me.

"I know he" — pointing from behind his back — "used to be Vic's boyfriend. My life was so much better when she was with you. She left me alone and messed with you instead." He glared at Hudson, then looked at me. "You must be the new girlfriend Vic was bitching about. She does **not** like you," he chuckled dryly.

"Amazingly enough, I figured that out myself," I replied just as dryly. "I'm guessing she doesn't like anybody but herself, family included." I shook my head in disgust. Just thinking about that woman made my blood boil. "Tell me your name. Like I said, I'm tired of saying hers."

"I don't blame you. Ugh, if she finds out I told you anything, I have no doubt that she'd kill me," his voice shook as he spoke, and he paled when he said that.

"We want to help you, but we need to understand everything. Your name first. How did you get involved in this? How'd Victoria find out about the gold? And why are you staying in the national forest?" Hudson added, "If you help us, we can help you and even offer you some support to get back on your feet. But you need to be honest with us. Tell us everything you know, and we'll do our best to protect you from her."

The brother hesitated for a moment before speaking, his guard slightly lowering. "My name's Tom. I didn't want any part in this. Vic insisted I help her find the gold, saying it would solve all our problems, but I'm sure what she really meant was only her problems. I'm not saying how she convinced me, but she got wind of it through something I found in an estate sale. I told her about it. I thought it was a joke, but... I swear I saw dollar signs in her eyes. As for staying in the forest, I've got nowhere else to go. I don't have any money to stay any place anymore."

Once Tom started talking, it was as if a dam had burst, and he spilled the entire story. He explained how he'd written the poems and flew the drone. He told us that, after Hudson and I had crossed to their side of the ravine, Victoria resorted to threats to make Tom leave.

She thought we were just stalling to try to figure out a way to keep it ourselves. But she'd severely underestimated the gold's weight. She believed she could move it on her own with no problems, Tom also told us that they were going to get the rest of the gold tomorrow. He said that she told him that she hid it, and he didn't know where it was. He also told us that Victoria had something important to do today, but she didn't tell him what it was.

"I guess that explains why the drone didn't bother us after that point," Hudson mused.

"Yeah... well... can you cut these cuffs off? They're starting to hurt."

My heart went out to him, but I shook my head gently. "I'm sorry, we can't do that," I said softly. "For a couple of reasons, but mostly because if Victoria happens to be in the park, it might work in our favor."

Hudson added, "She won't want any attention drawn to herself."

I went on to explain to Tom that the chances of him ending up in jail were slim to none. He would probably have to go through a psych evaluation, but they likely wouldn't do much either, but... I also told him it wasn't up to me what happened to him.

Hudson chimed in, "Once you're out of trouble, you can contact the Moose Creek Campground and RV Park and I'll help you, as long as Victoria is out of the picture." He paused and asked another question. "How come she didn't tell me she has a brother?"

Tom's voice wavered, laden with defeat. "She can't stand the idea that there's anybody smarter than herself. I really don't want to talk about her anymore," he said, his words saddened with the weight of the near-destruction Victoria had forced onto his life.

Hudson and I dropped him off at the ranger station and as much as I didn't want to, I wrote the report on what happened. Handing it to Benjamin's secretary, I left to finish the rest of my workday.

Hudson was waiting for me outside the ranger station. We walked toward the picnic area before we started talking. I sat across from him at the worn picnic table, the late afternoon sunlight filtering through the surrounding trees.

"So," I began, "I was supposed to start an environmental integrity study today. I'll be taking soil samples from the riverbanks. Benjamin was kind enough to postpone it until tomorrow because of the whole looking for Tom thing."

Hudson nodded, and his brow rose slightly. "I'm glad your boss did. I feel like we're a little closer to some answers.

I smiled and nodded, agreeing with him. " I just wish we were a lot closer, but it is what it is. Anyway, I'm going on the next Moon Walk Tour as a guest. Have you ever been on one? And do you want to go?"

Hudson's eyes lit up. "Yes! And they are worth it. The park, under a near or full moon, is incredible. I'd love to go again."

As we were discussing the details, Victoria sauntered over, her presence as unwelcome as a ticked-off rattlesnake. She slid onto the bench beside Hudson, her tone sugary sweet. "Hudson, baby, I can't believe we haven't spent any time together lately. You **must** have been so busy."

I clenched my teeth, silently seething. Hudson's response was sarcastically polite. "Sarah and I have been busy with everything that's happened. You know, dealing with false accusations. Cleaning up after the earthquake. Oh yeah, that one really interrupted us..." Hudson glanced at me and winked."

Victoria's jaw clenched behind her smile. Ignoring me entirely, she continued her attempt at charming him and completely ignoring what he just said. "Well, we should set up a date and do something about that. How about dinner tonight? Just the two of us?"

I exchanged a quick glance with Hudson, his eyes reflected the same confusion I felt. "I'll have to check my schedule," he replied flatly.

I forced a smile and bit my tongue. Our best chance of getting any information from her was from Hudson. But from her thorough disregard of what Hudson said, I knew she was up to something other than just a date. God! That bi... woman was already on my last nerve. Just what the heck was her game?

"Oh baby, stop teasing me. You know you want to enjoy a dinner with me and maybe afterward..." she said, implying something else entirely.

I was ready to jump across the table and slap her silly, but Hudson looked at me with a pleading look on his face. I didn't know if he was pleading for me to save him or for me to leave him. Maybe he thought he could get more information from her if he agreed to a date. Before I could let my mind wander too much towards something more negative, he cleared his throat.

Sitting up straight, Hudson's voice cut through the air like a thunderclap, sharp and uncompromising. "Victoria! Cut the crap! Were you not listening to what I said?" Rage radiated from him in tsunami-sized waves and Victoria, for a moment, seemed taken aback.

Her eyes narrowed, a storm of fury brewing within them. She clenched her fists, her face contorting into complete hatred. The polite facade shattered, revealing the true intensity of her emotions. "You don't get to talk to me like that," she hissed, her voice a venomous whisper. "You owe me, Hudson. Don't forget that."

The dangerous glint in her eyes was an unspoken threat lingering in the air. I could feel the tension crackling between them, a silent battle of wills that had been brewing for far too long. Whatever game Victoria was playing, it was clear that Hudson's patience was gone, and her attempts to manipulate him had hit an impenetrable wall.

As Victoria stood up, I braced myself for the storm that seemed inevitable, but to my surprise, she just turned and left. I watched her retreating figure, her steps uncertain as she hesitated near the forest's edge. She looked toward the forest, hesitating before she turned to face the parking area and walked in that direction.

"Well, that was anticlimactic," I said humorlessly.

Hudson, visibly relieved by her departure, shook his head, his expression a mix of irritation and resignation. I leaned in, curiosity getting the better of me. "Hudson, why does Victoria think you owe her?" My words came out as a whisper, my eyes locked onto his.

Hudson sighed, his shoulders sagging. "It's a long and complicated story, Sarah. But, in a nutshell, she believes I owe her because she helped me through a tough time a few years back. She helped me with a serious problem that I later found out she created, but she doesn't know that I know."

"What'd she do?" I asked in a hushed tone, shocked at her audacity.

He began with a deep sigh. "She made it seem like she rescued me from..." He looked down and took a deep breath. "A woman claimed I took advantage of her after she and I went on a date. I'd never even dated her in the first place. Victoria told me that she convinced the woman to back down by telling her that she would swear in court that Victoria and I were together the entire day it supposedly happened, or any other day she claimed.

"I can't even begin to tell you how grateful I felt toward her. I knew I hadn't done anything wrong, but just being accused..." He shook his head as if he couldn't believe it himself. "She made me think that she rescued me. Not long after that, we started dating. It was right before Victoria and I broke up, that the woman who supposedly accused me, came to me and told me that Victoria had threatened her to get her cooperation.

"Victoria wanted to be my savior. She wanted me to be in debt to her. And she held it over my head more than once too. The thing is, she doesn't know that I know she set up the whole thing."

My eyes widened and I covered my open mouth with my hand. That vile, sub-human's actions left me speechless for a moment. "Making up a lie like that could have ruined your life, and she's done it more than once now," I said in utter disbelief that anyone would do something like that.

# Chapter Twenty-Six

Hudson

The stress from Victoria's games must have been worse than I thought. I slept longer than I usually do and when I woke up, Sarah was already gone. Her spot on the bed had long since gone cold. I grabbed her pillow, cuddling it, but it was a poor substitute.

Groaning in frustration, I ached all over. Since the night Sarah and I found the gold Victoria hid, I've been on edge more than ever before. Victoria needed to be stopped.

Determined to find a way out of this mess, I picked up my phone and dialed Darren's number. As the call connected, I took a deep breath, preparing myself for the conversation we were about to have.

"Hey, Darren," I began, my tone cautious. "It's Hudson. I've got a... hypothetical situation I need your advice on. Let's say, for argument's sake, someone stumbles upon some gold, really old coins and bars, abandoned or maybe mislaid on their own land. What are the legalities around that?"

Darren's voice came through the phone, his tone serious. "Well, if it's abandoned, technically, it might be finders keepers. But mislaid gold, that's a different story. If the original owner can be found, they'll most likely get it. The law usually favors them. As for antiquated gold, it gets murky. If it's been hidden for a long, long time, chances are slim that anyone will come forward to claim it and you, hypothetically, could get to keep it."

"Would one hundred, ninety-three years be considered a long, long time?"

"That's an unusually specific amount of time, but hypothetically, I'd say yes. However, that's not for me to decide."

"Hypothetically speaking," I continued carefully, "what if someone started stealing parts of this gold, using threats to burn down the forest? How would you handle that situation?"

There was a brief silence on the other end, and then Darren's voice hardened. "That's a crime, no hypothetical about it. Extortion and theft. We'd launch an investigation immediately. We take that kind of threat seriously."

"And hypothetically, what would the person who found the gold need to do about the gold that was found?"

"You... whoever found the gold would need to turn it in to the police. We would investigate and might even need a court ruling as to what to do. What the courts decide would ultimately determine what happens." Darren laughed. "Any other hypothetical questions?"

I shook my head slowly. "No. Thanks, Darren. Just needed to clarify some things. Hypothetically, of course."

"Yeah, sure, Hudson," he replied, his tone slightly bemused. "Just let me know if you need any more... hypothetical advice."

I hung up, my mind swimming with the information. I still didn't know what to do. I knew I had to tread carefully, but I couldn't let Victoria win. If there was a way out of this, I was determined to find it.

I made a cup of coffee and thought about what to do, but after finishing it, I was no closer and decided to take a shower and then check to see if there was anything else I could do in the campground.

As I finished up the repairs in one of the cabins, I glanced around, ensuring everything that needed to be repaired was repaired. I cleaned up and looked at the bed. Intending to extend the life of the mattress, I decided to flip the mattress over. Pulling the mattress toward me, something hit the floor with a thud. A small, relatively new leather-bound book lay at my feet. Picking it up, I tossed it into my toolbox. I'd try to figure out who it belonged to later. After I sprayed the mattress with a disinfectant and finished cleaning the cabin, I headed back to my RV.

The book seemed inconspicuous enough, but when I opened its pages, I recognized Victoria's elegant handwriting immediately. Intrigued, I began reading. I seemed to be the subject of her journal. The pages detailed her thoughts and plans in intricate detail. My eyes scanned the words, and with each sentence, I felt my anger surge.

In those pages, her true intentions unfurled like a sinister plot in a thriller novel. She had meticulously outlined her scheme, her desperation to gain control over me, and her attempts to manipulate every situation to her advantage. It was chilling to see the extent she was willing to go, and the things she was willing to do in order to get what she wanted.

I realized the depth of her cunning and how she had played with my emotions and manipulated my trust. It was as if a veil had been lifted, revealing the ugly darkness behind her charming façade, and all of it... in her own words. Closing the diary, I clenched my fists as frustration coursed through me. How could I have been so blind? So stupid?

I tossed the journal in with the gold, making sure the hidden compartment was closed. As I stood, my phone buzzed. I glanced at the screen to find a message from Sarah reminding me about the Moon Walk tour, bringing a smile to my face. I quickly typed a response, assuring her I'd be there.

Noticing the time, I realized it was getting late and if I didn't hurry, I would be too. I stepped into the shower, the warm water relaxing my tense muscles. As good as it felt, I had to hurry. After drying off, I put cologne on. She may not have said so, but I knew Sarah liked the way I smelled and that brought a smile to my face.

Stepping out of my RV, I locked the door and got in my truck. After checking to make sure that the security system I recently installed was working, I drove off to meet Sarah at the Custer State Park Bison Center.

I pulled into the parking area and walked up to the large barn-like building. Sarah leaned on the railing, near the entrance doors. She'd changed out of her uniform and was wearing blue jeans, a lined blue jean jacket, and hiking boots. She looked sexy as hell! And I greeted her with a long hug, enjoying the feel of her body against mine.

The group leader gathered us together and began speaking with a slight drawl. "Ladies and gentlemen welcome to Custer State Park, home to one of the largest publicly owned bison herds in the nation. Unfortunately, you're about three weeks too early for the Buffalo Round-up. You might want to consider coming back then. It's really something amazing to see. During that time, the buffalo are rounded up and the animals are examined, branded, and culled to maintain the health of the herd. This park can only sustain around one thousand buffalo, so the excess animals are auctioned off.

"Bison are the largest land mammal in North America, with bulls weighing up to two thousand pounds and cows weighing up to one thousand. The calves are born between late March and May and nicknamed "red dogs" due to their orange-red color. As they grow, their fur darkens, and their characteristic hump and horns develop.

"Despite their size, bison are fast and agile, capable of reaching speeds up to 35 miles per hour. They can jump high fences and are strong swimmers. They feed primarily on grasses, weeds, and leafy plants, foraging anywhere from nine to eleven hours a day. They have extremely good senses of smell and hearing, which make up for their poor eyesight..."

While it was interesting, I'd been through this tour before. As we headed to the corrals, my mind wandered to what I hoped Sarah and I would be doing tonight. "Are you working tomorrow?" I asked softly. I hoped she wasn't. I wanted to spend the day in bed with her and make sure she couldn't walk right when we were done.

She turned her face in my direction, but her wide eyes continued to take in the sight of the huge animals. "Huh?"

I chuckled. "They are impressive, aren't they?"

"Uh-huh." Her eyes were glued to the bison as she spoke. "I want to see the round-up," she said in a whisper. "I've seen pictures and video, but in person..."

Placing my arm around her, I held on, afraid she might try to get close enough to touch one of them. "It's rutting season, the bulls are even more dangerous than usual." She was like a kid in a candy shop; all starry-eyed and not thinking clearly when she tried to get closer, but I held on.

As the tour was ending, the group leader said something about the gift shop closing in an hour, and Sarah practically dragged me there. She bought a T-shirt, a hoodie, and a baseball cap. Taking her purchases with her, we walked outside.

"I am so not used to this weather. It's freezing. Back in Texas, I'd be wearing shorts now. It didn't feel this cold when we were on the tour."

"You were too excited then. Let's go back to the RV. I'll get you all nice and toasty there."

Sarah was about to say something when my phone rang. I glanced at it and answered. "Hello."

"Hello Mr. West, this is Brandon with United Security Systems. We've detected an alarm at your residence indicating a possible break-in. The indoor camera has recorded an individual inside your home, and we are currently monitoring the situation. Are you inside your home now?"

"N... No." My voice shook. I never expected the system would ever be used. I waited for what seemed like forever for him to get back with me.

"Law enforcement has been notified and is on their way. I've informed the intruder that they are currently on camera and the authorities have been notified. I strongly advised her to leave the premises immediately, and informed her that her actions are being recorded," Brandon said in a business-like manner.

"I'm heading home now. Did she leave or is she still there?" I began running to my truck.

"She's still in your home and seems to be searching for something." He didn't say anything for a few minutes and then spoke to me again. "I've told the woman that the police are on the way, and she will be arrested, but she's still searching your home."

Starting my truck, the phone synced up with the navigation system and I was able to use the microphone in my truck. "How much longer until the police get to my home?" I said as I took off, dirt flying up from under the tires.

Brandon's voice came over the speakers. "They are three minutes out."

The winding road made me slow down almost as much as the threat of hitting something as big as a deer came into my mind. I doubted a deer would do much damage with the push bar attached to the front of my truck, but if it was something bigger, I could be in real danger.

The engine's hum was drowned out by the furious thoughts racing in my head as I drove back home through the night. I was grateful for the light of the nearly full moon. Gripping the steering wheel, my eyes darted between the road and the surrounding darkness, alert for any sign of movement.

I couldn't shake off the anger coursing through me. How could someone invade my space, my sanctuary? The audacity of anyone breaking into my home fueled a fire inside me that burned hotter than the raging furnace of my determination to protect what was mine. I gripped the steering wheel tighter and cussed the woman invading my home.

Beneath my anger, a nagging suspicion filled my mind. It had to be her — Victoria. Who else would be so brazen, so reckless? The very thought of her trespassing and then ignoring the fact the police were on their way, intensified my fury. As each mile passed, my grip on the wheel tightened.

# Chapter Twenty-Seven

Sarah

Anger and frustration surged through me as I stood dumbfounded and watched Hudson run to his truck and leave me there. The events of the night when we found the gold Victoria had hidden, still lingered in my mind like a persistent ghost, casting a shadow of doubt and insecurity over my thoughts. His reaction on the phone, the shock and then the fury etched on his face, only fueled my imagination with wild, unsettling possibilities.

I took a few deep breaths, gripping the steering wheel of my SUV, determined not to let my emotions spiral out of control. Insecurity gnawed at the edges of my confidence, but I did my best to not let it consume me. I told myself that there had to be a reasonable explanation for his behavior. Closing my eyes, I steadied my breathing and told myself to calm down. Starting the engine, I began the drive back to the RV park.

Flashing red and blue lights showed in the distance as I neared the entrance to the RV park. A sheriff's SUV blocked the way, stopping me in my tracks. Rolling the window down, I waved at the officer. "Excuse me, I'm staying in the RV park. Can I get through, please?"

"No, ma'am," he replied gruffly.

"Any idea how long this is going to take?" I asked, doing my best to keep the irritation out of my tone.

The sheriff eyed me suspiciously, his expression stern. "You'll be able to go in when we're done, ma'am," he said firmly, his words stoking the embers of my frustration.

Gripping the bottom of the wheel tightly, I was torn between waiting or leaving to find elsewhere to wait. Neither option sounded good to me.

As I sat there in my Tucson, the minutes crawled by like reluctant snails. Impatience gnawed at me, urging me to do something… anything. About half an hour had passed, and my frustration had reached its peak. I was just about to shift into reverse and find a coffee shop in Custer to wait when the sheriff's voice snapped me out of my head.

"Ma'am, back your vehicle out of the entrance. We're about to leave. You can go in after we're gone," he said in a firm tone.

With a nod, I backed out and waited another five minutes. A Sheriff's SUV pulled out of the RV park, followed by a second one and then the one blocking the drive left. I waited a bit longer to make sure that was all of them and then entered the park. Driving to Hudson's RV, I was met with the sight of him sitting in a chair outside of the RV, drinking a beer… or maybe I should say guzzling a beer. My footsteps were unusually tentative as I approached, uncertain of the storm brewing beneath his furrowed brow.

I settled down beside him and faced him. Hudson popped open another beer, the hiss of escaping gas punctuating the night. He didn't acknowledge my presence, his eyes fixed on some distant point beyond the horizon.

Tentatively, I reached out, my hand hovering in the air for a moment before finding its place on his arm. His skin was warm, but there was a chill in his gaze that sent shivers down my spine.

"Hudson," I said softly, searching for words that wouldn't make it worse. "What happened? Why were the police here?"

His jaw clenched, muscles bunching beneath my fingers. For a moment, I thought he wouldn't answer, but then he spoke.

"It was her. It was Victoria!" He said her name like it was corrosive acid. "She broke in and trashed the place! That bitch! She trashed my home!" he spat, his voice brimming with anger and frustration. Downing the rest of the bottle in his hand, he grabbed another one and opened it.

"If you want, I'll clean it up for you." I wanted to ease his mind, but I doubted it would be enough.

He looked at me as if I'd just arrived. "You want a beer?"

"Uh... sure..." I said drawing out the word. "Are you okay?"

Hudson grabbed another bottle out of the cooler, opened it, and handed it to me. The condensation chilled my fingers further. I took a sip of the cool liquid and then a deeper gulp. The taste was a little bitter and slightly hoppy, with a tang that teased my taste buds. As it slid down my throat, there was a brief burn, quickly replaced by a pleasant warmth that settled in my stomach.

The night air stung my face as I took a deep breath. I looked at Hudson. "So... are you going to tell me what's going on?" I asked, my voice steady despite the turmoil inside me. "Or do you want to drink more beer first?" I was fairly certain the sarcasm I didn't intend to come out, did.

Deep down, I knew the answer didn't matter anymore. I braced myself for his response, the ache of impending loss already settling in my chest. I guessed it really didn't matter. I was almost certain that whatever was going on between us was over. It would hurt at first, but I would get over it.

"Huh?" Hudson mumbled, his eyes glazed over from the alcohol haze that surrounded him.

I gritted my teeth, frustration seeping into my tone as I snapped at him. "Wake up!" My words were said quietly, but in a sharper tone than intended, laced with irritation born from hurt.

Taking a breath, I spoke at a normal level, trying to reach the part of him that seemed lost. "Are you going to tell me or not?" I continued. My words carried the weight of disappointment. "You know, I know we haven't known each other for very long, but I thought I meant something to you, but I guess not." I fought back the tears threatening to spill, refusing to let him see how much he was hurting me.

For a moment, it seemed like my words hung in the air, suspended between us. And then, as if waking from a stupor, Hudson's eyes sharpened with sudden realization.

"You do mean something to me," he said as if he just realized what I said. "You mean a lot to me. I don't understand where that's coming from. I'm dealing with more shit than I care to, and you say that?" his voice rose as he spoke.

Hudson's voice, though not loud, felt like a sharp blade slicing through me. "I see," I replied evenly, my tone belying the storm inside me. I turned and walked into the RV to pack my things. The chaos was extreme, it rivaled Tammy's rampage in the cabin next to the one I stayed in when I first came here. Still, I refused to let it distract me from what needed to be done.

Holding the tears back, I started packing my belongings. Hudson made no move to stop me, not even stepping inside the RV. Once again, I was grateful that all I had to pack was clothes and toiletries. In short order, I was ready to leave.

Exiting the RV, I began loading my SUV. Placing my bags in the back, I felt like this was just another ending to another failed relationship. As I shut the hatch door, I glanced at the RV where Hudson still sat, his expression unreadable. With a deep breath, I sat behind the wheel and pushed the start button. My tears wouldn't stop. I felt like such an idiot for trusting him.

Just as I was reaching for the seatbelt strap to buckle myself in, the door opened abruptly, startling me and Hudson pulled me out. His arms enveloped me, pulling me to his chest. He whispered desperately, "Don't go." My body shook as my tears fell uncontrollably. My arms hung limply by my sides, and I fought the urge to wrap my arms around him, but the battle was lost, and I found myself holding onto him tightly, my tears darkening his shirt.

"Give me another chance, please. I promise I won't mess it up again." His voice hitched as he spoke in a soft tone.

The storm inside me began to subside, but the hurt lingered. A deep ache in my heart seemed to echo throughout my body. I couldn't trust my voice, so I nodded into his chest.

He held me tighter when he felt the slight movement of my head. "Thank you."

Still holding onto me, Hudson reached into my Tucson and pressed the button to turn off the engine, his grip firm but gentle. Finding myself bent slightly backward in an awkward position, he grabbed my purse. I didn't mind as long as he didn't let go. The discomfort was overshadowed by the warmth of his arm around me, giving me the feeling of security I needed to feel right now.

"I'll explain everything. I think I was in shock after I saw the inside of my RV, but I don't want you to leave again." He went on to explain what he saw as she tore through the RV's contents, throwing things around simply because those things were meaningless to her.

My heart went out to him, having to deal with someone tearing apart his home. "You didn't have to deal with this alone the last time and you don't have to deal with this alone this time either. Hudson… I offered to help." A thought hit me. "Wait… did they catch her and arrest her, or did she get away?"

"I was talking with the guy from the security company while she was still inside. He told me that he warned her multiple times to get out, but she ignored him and kept on tearing the place apart. She only stopped when the police stopped her."

"Did she try to take anything or was she just here to trash the place?"

His voice was steady, though a hint of pain still lingered in his words. "She didn't take anything, but I think I know what she was looking for."

Hudson went on to explain about the diary he found in the cabin where she stayed. He told me about the plans she made, some already executed and some still in the works. As he spoke, I felt horror at the level of depravity in her psyche and anger at her for destroying his home.

"I have the diary," Hudson continued, his calm expression masked the pain he must be feeling. "You can read it if you want and see for yourself what she intended to do."

I nodded, almost afraid of what she wrote and what her intentions were. He took my hand and led me into the RV. Seeing the mess she created, as if for the first time, shocked me. This time, I wasn't in a rush to get out and the disaster she left in her wake brought tears to my eyes.

Hudson's face paled the longer he was inside. My heart ached to see him like that, and I couldn't bear it any longer. I stopped him and told him that we needed to clean up first. His shoulders sagged and he looked more dejected than the first time we cleaned up the mess that Tammy created and then the mess from the quake. It was as if the thought of cleaning up again was just too much to handle.

"Okay, look, the bedroom isn't too bad, why don't you wait in there and I'll clean up."

"Thank you, but no. This is my home. But I would really appreciate it if you would help me. At this point, I can't believe you even stayed, but I'm so glad you did. There's no telling what's going to get torn up next." The irritation and sadness in his voice were clear, and it seemed as if he was ready to throw in the towel.

Hudson pulled me into a comforting hug, kissing the top of my head. "For now, let's just clean a space to sit and talk. I might be drinking another beer." Rubbing my back, he continued to hold me. The warmth of his body and the feel of his arms around me eased my mind and calmed my heart.

# Chapter Twenty-Eight

### Hudson

I didn't want to let her go. I wanted to hold Sarah until I woke up from this nightmare. The longer we stood there like that, the more I wanted to stay like that. She felt so good, so right, in my arms, pressed against me.

She sighed. "As nice as this is, it's not getting any of the cleaning done." But she didn't let go either. "I don't think the housekeeping fairies are going to do this for us."

I chuckled and she looked up at me, her face flushed pink with a grin that warmed my entire body. "The quicker we get this done, the quicker you can take a look at her journal, and we can make a plan about what to do."

We spent the next hour cleaning the broken glass, washing dishes that weren't broken, putting them away, and salvaging what we could. I plugged in the Keurig machine and hoped it still worked. The room looked leagues better, but the coffee maker didn't' survive.

"Well, that sucks," Sarah said in a sad tone. "I'm going to miss it."

Wrapping my arms around her, I laughed. "I'll get us another one." I sat, pulling her down on my lap. "You ready to read it?"

She nodded, but then I realized it meant she'd have to move from this position, and I didn't want to go get it. I took a deep breath; it was now or never. "Come on, it's in the bedroom." Begrudgingly, I stood.

Retrieving the journal from its hiding place, handed it to her, and sitting on the bed, she began reading. The further she got into it, the more she mumbled to herself saying, "Oh, my," "Unbelievable," "Wow," "She's deluded," and "She's just... twisted."

Sarah finished reading and handed the journal to me. Her hands were shaking, and she looked pale. "I am... I am... so sorry. I had no idea what she did to you. She's genuinely warped. What are you going to do about it?"

"Tomorrow, or I guess I should say later today, I'm going to call Darren and talk to him. Right now, I just want to forget about everything that has to do with her. I'm just tired." I laid on the bed and closed my eyes.

Bolting upright in bed, my heart pounded, the remnants of a nightmare faded like mist in the morning sun. The space beside me was empty, the sheets cool to the touch. Panic clawed at my chest. Where was she? Did she leave? Did she decide I wasn't worth the trouble?

I stumbled out of bed, my mind racing with a thousand insecurities. Maybe I'd pushed her too far, and she'd finally had enough. As I hurried into the kitchen area, dread gnawed at me. The sight of the empty kitchen intensified my fears. I cursed myself for the fool I'd been, for letting someone as incredible as her slip through my fingers.

Just as despair threatened to consume me, the door creaked open, and there she was, carrying two cups of coffee and wearing a smile that could light up the darkest room. Relief washed over me like a tidal wave, leaving me feeling weak, but grateful.

"Morning," she said, her voice light and happy, and suddenly the day felt brighter and more hopeful. "I thought you might like one of these." She handed the warm cup to me.

I barely managed a small smile, my voice catching in my throat. "Morning," I replied, taking the cup from her. The fear that gripped me began loosening its hold. "I thought you... I thought you left."

"Oh... You mean like left and wasn't coming back. Why would I leave?" she asked, her eyes searching mine, and at that moment, I knew I didn't want to be without her, ever.

"I don't know. I've just... messed up so much. I thought maybe you'd had enough," I admitted, my voice rough with emotion.

She placed her delicate hand over mine from across the table, her touch was warm and reassuring. "We all make mistakes, Hudson," she said gently. "What matters is that we learn from those mistakes, do better, and not make them again. I'm here because I want to be, despite everything. I... I want to be here... with you."

Her words cut through my doubts, injecting hope into my soul. I tightened my grip on her hand. "I want you to be here too," I said, my voice steadier now.

• ♥ • ♥ • ♥ • ♥ • ♥ •

Darren sat across from Sarah and me. The smirk on his face confused me until he started talking. "I'm glad you called. I want to see what you hypothetically found."

"First," — I pushed the journal toward him. — "I think this is what she was looking for. I found it in the cabin she stayed in when I was cleaning it after the quake."

Opening it, he began to read. Sarah and I watched as his eyes grew large. When he closed it, he whistled a long whistle. "Damn. She's... Did you really find gold like she said? Or is this just the deluded ramblings of a psychopath?"

"Yeah, Sarah and I did." Sarah squeezed my hand and leaned closer to me.

"You know I'll have to take this with me, and it's going to get out that there's gold bars and coins on your land. You could have a real problem with opportunistic treasure hunters swarming your land," Darren's compassion was evident as he spoke, but then his expression hardened as he continued. "Where is the gold now?"

I glanced at Sarah; her warm smile gave me strength. "Some of it's here in the RV," I said, my voice steady despite the turmoil inside me. "We don't know where Victoria hid what she took, but the rest is still where we found it."

Darren's gaze flickered between us, calculating the risks. "You need to understand the gravity of this situation," he said, his tone grave. "We can't risk this information leaking prematurely. The consequences for you could be severe."

I nodded, my mind racing with dangers. "We know, but will you give us some time? Let us retrieve the rest of the gold so we can turn it all in at the same time. That way it would be in police custody and safer than it being here."

Darren sighed, the lines on his face deepening with the burden of his decision. After what seemed like an eternity, he finally relented. "Fine but you'll need to make it quick. I can give you two days and I'm going to need the journal back. The District Attorney's Office is going to want this when it comes to prosecuting Victoria. For now, I'll leave the journal with you — be grateful I consider you a friend. If you screw me over… But remember, time is not on your side."

After Darren left, I looked at Sarah. "Will you help me look for the gold Victoria took? I doubt she carried them very far. Knowing her, she was probably planning on using her brother to do the heavy lifting. What I don't understand is why she told her brother about the coins. They don't weigh that much and are worth a lot of money. It doesn't make sense to me." I was genuinely curious about her way of thinking.

Sarah looked down at the table and spoke softly. "Are you sure you want me to help? I don't want to…" Her voice shook and she didn't look at me.

I scooted next to her and put my arm around her. Kissing her temple, I pulled her to me. "I promise I want your help. I trust you. I know you're not her. I'm sorry if I made it seem like I thought you were."

Gently turning her face toward me, I looked her in the eyes and placed a tender kiss on her lips. When I picked her up and put her on my lap, I swear, she squeaked. It was so cute, I laughed and held her close to my chest. She inhaled deeply and wrapped her arms around me. This… felt right.

"Will you help me?" I whispered in her ear. She nodded in reply, but we didn't move. I wanted to sit here longer. No, I wanted her in my bed. But, as Darren put it, time wasn't on our side. "As much as I want to stay here with you, we only have two days. Are you ready to go?"

She exhaled and her entire body slumped. "I guess so," she said in a disappointed tone.

We grabbed our backpacks and headed off. At least it was daytime. It should be easier this time.

We followed the trail back to where we found the chest of gold Victoria had hidden. Searching through the dense undergrowth, my eyes scanned the familiar terrain as I poked leaf piles and looked under rock piles. We searched for over an hour and found nothing.

I couldn't shake the image of Victoria struggling under the weight of those gold bars. They were heavy and cumbersome. She wouldn't have gone too far with them. It wasn't like her to do any heavy lifting herself. It had to be near where the chest was found.

The forest seemed to close in around us, the dense foliage and trees cast shadows on the forest floor. As we ventured deeper, I felt determined. I wasn't going to let Victoria win and get her hands on my property. The gold was here somewhere; it had to be. Sarah, a short distance from me, moved with purpose, her eyes scanned the forest floor.

"We're close," I whispered to her, my voice barely audible over the sounds of the forest. "I can feel it."

Sarah grunted in pain and hopped on one foot for a few seconds. "Ow, ow, ow, ow. F... found it." Despite the pain, she laughed. "Next time, you get to kick the gold. She covered it with a bunch of leaf litter."

I rushed to her side to make sure she was okay, and she looked at me with a mischievous grin. "Are you okay?"

She beamed. "Let's pack this... stuff and get out of here. Thank God there's only three of them this time." She looked at me and smiled. "At least you got all of the bars back. She still has six of the coins, but... it's better than nothing."

I carried two and Sarah carried one of the bars in our packs. We moved quickly to get back to the RV and relative safety. This time, I showed Sarah where all the gold was. "There's one more thing we need to do, and I don't know how we're going to be able to do it."

"What's that?"

"We need to get the rest of the gold out of that cave."

Sarah looked at me surprised. "What do you mean you don't know how? It's simple."

I looked at her incredulously in return. "How is it simple? I don't know about you, but I don't want to carry that much gold again. And... it needs to be finished by tomorrow."

"Then I guess, we need to go to town right now."

Her beautiful smile distracted me with ideas that had nothing to do with gold. "What does going to town have to do with anything?"

"Well, unless you already have an ATV here, you need one. I am all for letting a machine carry that weight. You know, since we don't have to jump a ravine to cross to the other side. We can just ride across, and it will be so much faster."

"Oh..." Why didn't I think of that? "You know, in my defense, when I'm around you, my brain doesn't always work... in that way." I could feel the heat rise to my face. Since I first screwed up, we hadn't done more than kiss, and I wanted more from her.

Her eyebrows shot up and in a playful way asked, "Really? And how, exactly, does your brain work when I'm around?" She put her elbows on the table, laced her fingers together, and rested her chin on them, smiling the whole time.

When I didn't answer, she cocked her head to the side and smiled wider. When I still didn't answer, she stood up and walked around the table to my side. I scooted to the edge of the bench seat, wrapped my arms around her, and pulled her to me. My face was buried in her chest, her firm breast pressed against my cheeks, and the low moan coming from her excited me.

Her fingernails gently raked through my hair, grazing my scalp as she straddled my legs and sat on them. She placed her hand on my cheek and leaned in to kiss me. I liked this side of her; the side that told me she wanted me.

# Chapter Twenty-Nine

### Sarah

Placing my hand on his cheek, I leaned in to kiss him. Just as our lips touched, his phone rang, startling me. I jumped and had to laugh at myself. Hudson grinned at me and gave me a quick peck on my lips.

When he checked to see who was calling, he answered. "Hey, Darren. What's up?... I know... I know... Yes, we're working on it... Okay, I promise... Bye."

He looked a bit dejected. "As much as I would like to continue with what we were doing, we need to go to town."

I didn't want to stop what we'd started, and my heart sank a little when Hudson mentioned we needed to go to town. "What did Darren want? And why are we going to town?"

"He called to remind me about the deadline." His eyebrows furrowed. "Did you forget already? Maybe your brain doesn't work right when you're around me either. We need an ATV or two. Raincheck?" He waggled his brows.

"We **will** absolutely continue this later," I assured him. I tried to get off his lap, but he wouldn't let me. He held me tightly and placed a soft kiss on my lips.

"Absolutely." His low, husky voice was so seductive.

"Um... I'm going to need to use the restroom before we go." I doubt he knew what he'd done to me already.

•♥•♥•♥•♥•♥•

Having purchased two full-sized Rhino 250 utility four-wheelers, we walked out of the store and headed to the next place to buy a trailer. Hudson purchased a trailer large enough to carry the four-wheelers. We were in and out of town within four hours and were back at the RV, trailer in tow.

These four-wheelers could carry up to five hundred pounds and we would need that to get the gold back. I was looking forward to this trip, it was going to be so much easier than the other three trips considering we would be carrying a lot more weight this time.

We quickly got ready to go, strapping a five-gallon tank of gas on Hudson's four-wheeler and the backpacks on mine. Putting on our helmets, we took off. I followed him and we bounced along, sometimes going fast, sometimes slow, having to create our own trail through the underbrush. But riding was so much better.

Dust swirled behind Hudson, and I was so grateful the helmet stopped most of it from me breathing it in. Once we reached the cross-over point, we'd been riding for only twenty-two minutes. Thank God for these four-wheelers! Within another half hour, we were standing at the rock face and entrance to the cave.

Hudson pulled off his helmet, and a huge grin covered his entire face. God, that man's gorgeous! My smile matched his.

"That... was fun!" he said through his smile. "We wouldn't even be a quarter of the way here if we'd been walking. You" — he grabbed my shoulders and pulled me to him, kissing me — "had the best idea! Come on. Let's get the gold and go back home."

Pocketing the ATV keys and taking our backpacks, we walked to the cave entrance, his arm around my shoulder and mine around his waist. He entered first and I followed. Once we were both inside the first cavern, Hudson lifted me up to the ledge and I crawled through the opening of the tunnel to the next cavern.

I stood, surveying the beauty of this cavern once again. It felt like I was on another planet, even though I'd seen it before, it still took my breath away. Crystals in the rock reflected the light from my flashlight, creating tiny, pinpricks of lights everywhere. The only word that even came close to describing it was magnificent, and I was in awe of the natural splendor surrounding me again.

"Not to rush you Sarah, but we need to get everything and get out of here. If... you remember, we have a raincheck to take care of. Nothing, and I mean nothing, is going to stop me from redeeming it." Hudson picked me up and I wrapped my legs around him.

His kiss was hot and passionate. Our tongues swirled around each other in perfect harmony. This kiss felt different. It felt like... so much more. If he had even hinted at more than just the kiss, I couldn't have said no. I wanted him.

Setting me down slowly, the kiss continued, but reluctantly, we parted. The kiss didn't last long enough. "You don't know what you do to me, Sarah."

"Uh, probably it's close to what you do to me." I was breathing hard, and heat radiated from every pore of my body.

"Good."

We worked as fast as we could, making multiple trips to the ledge and back before we retrieved all the bars and coins. Carrying six bars and forty coins without the chest was much more difficult, and we fought to carry them one at a time through the tunnel. Beads of sweat trickled down our faces the longer we struggled with the challenging task.

One at a time the bars were lowered to the first chamber and then out the entrance tunnel. We strapped our heavy packs to the back of the ATVs and topped off the gas tanks.

The bars probably only weighed about twenty-five pounds each but carrying them for hours was another story. Thank God for modern machines!

We pulled up to the RV, the sun was setting, creating long, dark shadows across the landscape, and took the backpacks in. A quick series of loud metallic 'thunks' sounded as I started to set down the pack I was carrying. The strap had torn completely away from the pack, creating a large tear in the material.

"Are you okay?" Hudson rushed to me, nearly shouting at the top of his lungs.

I sighed heavily. "Yes, I'm good. I guess I won't be using this anymore. Damn," I mumbled. "I really liked that one."

"Thank God. Uh... I'll get you another one, just as good or even better than that one."

I couldn't contain it; laughter bubbled up from within me. It began as a gentle rumble, my shoulders trembling, but quickly escalated into uncontrollable laughter. "Just an inch more, and my foot would've been history!" I managed to choke out between fits of giggles.

"Sarah! That's not funny! You could've been seriously hurt." Hudson scolded me, but concern filled his voice.

Tears ran down my cheeks as I struggled to stifle my laughter, covering my mouth with my hand. "But I wasn't, and honestly, I think I'm just too tired to think straight. All I want right now is a shower.

"No raincheck tonight, huh?" he said sounding saddened.

"I'll let you know after I feel clean again," I replied, the humor had drained from my voice, leaving behind only weariness and the anticipation of a warm shower.

"I'll put the gold away and take a shower after you. Try not to use all the hot water." He winked and smiled, but the disappointment was still in his voice.

After washing the sweat and grime off, my mood improved dramatically. I was ready to go and ready to collect on the raincheck. Hudson went in after and when he was done, he seemed to be in a much happier mood. Just as he walked into the kitchen area, his phone rang.

Hudson begrudgingly answered when he saw that it was Darren. Darren must have had a lot to say because all Hudson kept saying was "Mm-huh," "Uh-huh," "I understand," and "Okay, yeah, I'll leave now."

"Damn it!" he spat. "I was feeling so much better after that shower too. Victoria's arraignment's been moved up to tomorrow morning at nine-thirty. Darren said it's now or never to get that diary to him. If you don't feel like going, I'll go by myself," he explained, frustration filling his words.

"I don't mind going. I mean, if you want me to go, I will."

Hudson looked at me with appreciation and he smiled, but there was something else in his smile that caught me off guard. I hoped it wasn't wishful thinking on my part. I've been wrong before and I regretted it. In Hudson's case, it would hurt too much if I was wrong.

"Hey! At least we smell nice now," I quipped with a goofy grin.

"Come on. Let's get this over with." Hudson pulled me into a hug. "You do smell nice," he said as he rubbed my back. His hand went lower and lower and…

"If we don't leave now, we're not going." This needed to stop if we were going to make it to the sheriff's office today.

Hudson's grin lit up his entire face. Kissing my forehead, he said, "I'm thinking. I'm thinking. Ugh! Let's go." His frustration matched mine, but we went anyway.

· ♥ · ♥ · ♥ · ♥ · ♥ ·

Darren met us at the reception desk; relief that we brought the journal showed on his face as Hudson handed it to him. As we stood there chatting, a cacophony of high-pitched screams pierced the hushed atmosphere, sending a chill down my spine. It sounded like a woman was being brutally murdered.

Startled, all three of us turned toward the source of the commotion. Darren approached the Sally Port door cautiously. His hand gripped the handle, and as he pulled it open, a gust of wind rushed in as the door swung violently open with such force that Darren stumbled backward and hit the ground; an audible grunt escaped him.

Like a nightmarish creature, Victoria burst through the doorway, her eyes wild and frenzied. Her disheveled hair clung to her face, and the crazed look in her eyes chilled me to the bone. Time seemed to slow as she advanced like an insane woman. A surge of fear shot through me like a bolt of lightning and my heartbeat doubled.

Hudson's strong arms pulled me behind his solid frame. I could feel the tension in his muscles as he shielded me, blocking my view of Victoria. Her screams reverberated through the air, each one sending a shockwave of fear through me. They were filled with vile words about her wanting to kill me and that it was my fault that Hudson wouldn't give her another chance.

Through the jostling of Hudson's body, I could sense the frantic energy of her attacks, each assault causing Hudson to shift, pushing me back slightly with every blow. She was unhinged, a wild beast hell-bent on destroying me and everything in her path. Despite her unhinged frenzy, Hudson stood firm, absorbing the brunt of her assaults and saving me from her fury. I stepped back far enough to witness the anarchy.

Amid the turmoil, two officers emerged from the Sally Port door. One with a bloodied nose, and the other with a scratched and bloodied cheek. Their faces were a mask of anger and caution, knowing they were facing the insane woman who'd injured them.

Together, they approached her from behind, each grabbing one arm. Their vice-like grip stopped her from clawing at Hudson, but that left her legs free, and she kicked and screamed at both Hudson and me. With a quick kick to the back of her knee, Victoria was on the ground, her cheek on the floor.

Still, she fought as if her life depended on it, but after so much effort, her strength gave out. Her body went limp as she was cuffed. Not taking any chances, the officer with the scratched cheek also cuffed her ankles. Her gravelly voice still protested, but now it was not much more than a shadow of its former self.

Once she'd been secured and unable to attack anyone again, Hudson turned around and asked me in a panicked voice if I was okay. I was breathing heavily and shaking more than ever. I nodded but couldn't speak.

"Would someone get some water, please?" Hudson spoke in a calm, soft voice. "She won't bother anyone again. They've taken her away." He slowly rubbed my back as he spoke.

I nodded again. Looking at Hudson's arms, my eyes grew wide. Long, ugly scratches covered his arms. Blood oozed from them, and I finally snapped out of my stupor.

"Your arms..." my voice shook as I spoke. Covering my mouth with a shaking hand, I swallowed hard. "Hudson... Oh my God! She would have... Oh my God. I'm so sorry. It's all my fault. Oh my God. I'm so sorry," I choked out between sobs.

"I'm fine. If you would've been hurt... Don't worry about me. As long as you're okay, that's all that matters."

His tender words moved me to more tears, and I threw my arms around his neck and held on for dear life.

Paramedics arrived and tended to the three men Victoria attacked. Hudson was helped last — probably because we wouldn't let go and held tightly to each other. The longer he held me, the better... no, the safer I felt.

Once Hudson had been taken care of and bandaged up, we spoke with Darren. They were going to have her committed for observation at a psychiatric hospital. He told us that with everything that happened, and it all being caught on video, she might be there a long time. I felt like I could finally breathe again.

# Chapter Thirty

Hudson

We sat at the kitchen table, just trying to relax, but, and I didn't want to admit it, my arms were stinging like crazy. Victoria scratched me up pretty badly. I'm glad I stopped her from getting at my face, but damn! The only thing I was grateful for was that Sarah didn't get hurt. If she had, I would have never forgiven myself.

"I feel so awful that you got hurt." Sarah stood up and then sat on my lap facing me, straddling my legs. Putting her hands on my shoulders, she looked me straight in the eyes. "I've been scared before, but never like that. And at the same time, I've never felt safer. It was so surreal. If it weren't for you... Well, I'm sure she would have really hurt me." She placed a soft, lingering kiss on my lips. "You make me feel safe, Hudson."

I swelled with pride. That had to be the best compliment I'd ever gotten. No one had ever said something like that to me before. It made me feel useful and appreciated. "When it comes to you, that's my job. I'll always protect you, Sarah. Even if I do stupid things sometimes, I'll always keep you safe."

"Did she hurt you anywhere else besides your arms?"

"Thankfully no. When they stop stinging so much, I hope that will be tomorrow, I'm going to collect on that raincheck and I swear to you, nothing's going to stop me." Even if my arms still hurt, I wouldn't say so. I'm going to show her how I feel about her, for as long, and as many times as possible.

• ♥ • ♥ • ♥ • ♥ • ♥ •

Sarah came home from work with a huge smile on her face, brimming with excitement that was contagious. "You won't believe what happened today," she exclaimed, overflowing with enthusiasm. "I've been chosen to help with a biodiversity survey in the park!"

Her joy was palpable, and I couldn't help but grin in response. "That sounds amazing. It sounds like it's right up your alley. Tell me all about it."

She eagerly launched into an explanation, her words tumbling out in a rush. "I'm hoping to spot some of the lesser seen species, like the Black-Footed Ferret, it's endangered but coming back, and the Swift Fox. Oh, and I'm crossing my fingers for a glimpse of a Northern Goshawk. The only thing I'm not looking forward to seeing is another Mountain lion. Once was enough."

She may have said she didn't want to see one, but I would bet money that she'd still be happy if she did.

"I'll be out there for a few nights," she continued, her eyes sparkling with anticipation. "I asked if only rangers are allowed to go and of course, they said yes, but... Benjamin told me that no one can stop anyone from camping in the park. Please say you like camping and you really want to go."

A mischievous glint danced in her eyes, and I chuckled. Camping under the stars, surrounded by the sounds of nature, with Sarah there — that was my kind of adventure. "As a matter of fact, I love camping. Camping that doesn't involve any heavy lifting in any way. When's it happening and who else is going with you?"

"This is just an initial study, to get a better idea of what's out there, what's going on, collect data, and of course do the not nearly as fun paperwork. There will be a more involved study after the initial findings give us an idea of what's going on. But... it starts next Monday, and it'll last for three days. After I get back, they're sending another ranger out for another three days to a different location. They want to see what kinds of information different people collect from other locations. I'm so excited!"

Sarah was brimming with anticipation. Her radiant smile. Her sparkling eyes. The joy she emitted; she was the most beautiful woman I'd ever seen. Her passion for nature rivaled my own and I wanted to help her in any way I could.

By the weekend, Sarah's growing restlessness with the excitement of her upcoming biodiversity survey seemed to be overwhelming her. The crackling energy around her was intense, and I could tell she needed a distraction. I also wanted to get her opinion on an area I'd been considering as a new home site.

Walking along a trail Sarah had not been on before, I did my best to talk about anything but her upcoming study. We arrived at a spot with a breathtaking view, the sun's golden rays lit up the landscape. The mountains to the west set a serene backdrop to the area and a sense of calm filled my soul.

I watched her face as I asked, "What do you think of that view?" Her opinion would help me decide, one way or the other.

"It's amazing," she said as she looked starstruck, taking in the view. "This is so beautiful. Imagine waking up and seeing this every day." Not taking her eyes off what was before her, her expression was one of wonderous awe.

"Well, we can come up here whenever you like." A smile covered my face as excitement ran through my body, and I made up my mind. This would be the spot.

It was starting to get darker, and we began heading back to the RV. I could barely contain my excitement for my plans, but then worry filled my mind. Insecurities from past experiences occupied my thoughts and all the "what-ifs" bombarded me.

Sarah thanked me for taking her to see that amazing view, and I was off, in my own little world, worrying about everything. When she turned to look at me and saw the concern on my face, she stopped and asked what was wrong.

I had to think of something quick, so I lied. "I was just wondering, what exactly does a biodiversity study involve? I mean, I don't want to get in your way and mess things up for you. Are you sure it's okay if I go with you?"

"Of course, it's okay. This first part is basically a search mission. We're supposed to find where the animals are, so we'll probably be doing a lot of walking and probably not a lot of talking. I just have to get GPS coordinates and list which animal is in that area. If possible, I need to find its den, nest, or range and report it. After we're done with the initial finding, then the actual study will take place.

"As for you being in the way, I don't think that's possible. Benjamin doesn't really want to send any of us alone, but the budget says otherwise. So, he told us that if we could get someone to go with us, it would make him feel better about it. Plus, Benjamin said I can use one of the Gators. You do… want to go with me, don't you? Have you changed your mind? If you don't, you need to tell me." She looked upset that I might not want to go with her.

"No, no, no! I want to go with you. I promise. I absolutely promise I want to go." I was being stupid. Sarah wasn't like Victoria. If I reacted like the last time, I would definitely screw things up with her. I just needed to take a breath and hang in there. I knew Sarah was different and I had to keep telling myself that.

As I went to put an arm around her shoulder, I rubbed one of the deeper scratches the wrong way and I jerked my arm back. I groaned quietly, but Sarah heard.

"Come on. When we get back home, you need to let me take a look at your arms. I wish I could do more to help you heal faster." She hugged me tightly. I loved the feeling of her body against mine. I just wish clothes weren't in between us.

### Sarah

I wanted it to be Monday already, not Friday. I wanted to start the study, but it was still three days away. I was excited beyond belief. The only thing that was putting a damper on it was Hudson being hurt. I wanted him to feel up to coming with me and not have any problems doing it.

The day moved along much faster than I thought it would and just as I was about to walk out of the ranger station, Benjamin stopped me and asked me to follow him to his office.

I sat in Benjamin's office, my palms slightly clammy despite the chill in the air. His stern expression sent shivers down my spine. I couldn't think of anything I'd done wrong. As I waited for him to speak, the silence in the room grew heavier, suffocating me.

"Sarah," Benjamin began, his voice measured but laced with disappointment, "I'm afraid I have some bad news. Due to a funding cut, we have to cancel the biodiversity study."

His words hit me like a sledgehammer. Canceled? A dream project, the chance to make a real difference for the park. I'd already packed almost everything, and all of it just vanished in an instant. I tried to swallow the lump in my throat, my eyes widening in disbelief. "But... but why?" I managed to stammer, my voice barely a whisper.

Benjamin's expression softened, but the anger was still there. "They said it was due to budget constraints," he said, his gaze flickering away for a moment before meeting mine again. "What the rangers here could do for the study isn't the problem. It's all the extra people who would need to be here for it. They probably needed their offices redecorated for all I know. Damn it! That was so important for this park!"

I felt hot, stinging tears welled up. I nodded; my throat too tight to speak. My mind was in a daze, and I made my way out of his office. Each step felt like I was trudging through quicksand. The weight of my shattered dream pressed down on me, threatening to crush me beneath its finality.

Somehow, I made my way to my Tucson through blurred vision. As I sat in the driver's seat, I let the emotions wash over me. Grief, frustration, and an overwhelming sense of loss engulfed me. My hand shook as I pushed the start button. It took all my strength just to back out of the parking space.

Through the veil of my tears, the road back to Hudson's RV blurred into a kaleidoscope of colors. I parked in my usual spot and killed the engine. I couldn't move. The disappointment was too much.

A gentle knock on my window shattered the stillness, making me jump. I turned to see Hudson; his face etched with concern. I opened the door, my voice catching in my throat. "They canceled the study," I managed to say through my tears.

Hudson's eyes softened with compassion. "Come here," he said as he pulled me to his chest and wrapped me in a warm embrace. "Did they say why?" he said softly. I nodded my head yes. "Is there a possibility that they'll start it up again at some time?"

"I don't know. Benjamin said they said it was a funding cut. Ugh! I'm sorry. I usually don't get so upset about stuff like this. It's happened before and I didn't get like this. I don't know what's wrong with me."

Hudson softly chuckled. "You've been through a lot lately. Don't beat yourself up. Let's go inside. You must be cold. We'll break in the new Keurig."

The aroma of coffee filled the small space, and I gratefully sipped the hot beverage. "You've been through a lot too, and you're not crying like a baby." Of course, he wouldn't cry, he's a man. A wonderful, masculine, gorgeous man. "How's your arms?"

"Much better. A few more days and it should be all better." His smile was beautiful.

# Chapter Thirty-One

Hudson

Taking a deep breath, I hoped what I was about to tell Sarah wouldn't make things worse. "I got a call from Darren earlier. Do you want me to tell you about it?"

She chuckled wryly. "Depends. Is it good news or bad news? Oh, never mind that. Tell me. I'll put my big girl panties on. Go ahead."

I raised an eyebrow. "Really? Can I watch?" I said, waggling my eyebrows.

Her eyes opened wide for a second and then she started laughing. "I would have thought you'd rather watch me take them off." She immediately turned beet red as she covered her mouth with both hands.

"Yeah, that too." She looked so cute when she embarrassed herself. My jaw started hurting from how much I was smiling.

She tried to stifle her laughter as she spoke. "Are you going to tell me or not?"

"Okay, it's good news. It doesn't look like we'll have to deal with Victoria for a long time. Considering what was in the journal, her run-in with the sheriff's officers and me, her threat of burning down the forest, the theft, and the false claims of assault, she'll be behind bars for a while. She also has to attend counseling sessions twice a week for the next five years and then weekly after that for however many years before she's even eligible for parole. Her attorney convinced her to take the deal. If she didn't, she'd probably be in prison for longer."

It looked like Sarah had been holding her breath as I told her, and when I finished, she slowly exhaled. "I can't believe it... that's amazing news! I'm guessing it's because of the theft. I mean, old gold coins could be worth a ton."

I was about to agree with her when my phone rang. Answering, I spoke with the architect. The floor plans were ready for approval or changes. "I have to go somewhere. Do you want to come with me?"

"Now? O... Okay, as long as it's not the Sheriff's Office." She winked.

We headed to Custer and parked in front of a building that looked like a log cabin. The only thing that made it different from a regular house was the double glass entrance doors. Knocking on the glass door, the light came on and the door was unlocked for us.

Jerry greeted me warmly, his eyes lighting up with enthusiasm. "Hudson, come in. I think you'll like what I've got so far. If you see something you want changed, just let me know."

I nodded appreciatively, my eyes scanning the preliminary sketches Jerry handed to me. The design looked promising, but I wanted Sarah's input. Just as I was about to speak, Jerry's eyes flickered past me and widened in surprise.

"I didn't know you were bringing someone, Hudson," Jerry said, with a curious tone.

I turned, a proud smile curving my lips. "Jerry, meet Sarah," I said, gesturing towards her. "Sarah, this is Jerry. Jerry and I went to high school together.

Sarah offered him a warm smile as Jerry extended a hand, his surprise transforming into genuine interest. Seeing Jerry's reaction to Sarah, I felt my pride swell and a little bit too much protectiveness. He'd better be glad he was a good architect because he was nearly drooling over Sarah and for anybody else, that would have earned him a punch to the gut.

"What are you drawing for Hudson?" Confusion filled her expression.

"A house." Now Jerry was very confused.

Sarah stood beside me, her gaze sweeping over the blueprints spread across the architect's desk. My excitement bubbled beneath the surface as I turned to her.

"Sarah, I've decided to have a house built," I said, watching her eyes light up with surprise and intrigue. "I thought it was time."

She blinked, clearly taken aback, her confusion etched on her face. "But why ask me about it?" she wondered aloud.

"Because your opinion matters to me," I replied honestly, my eyes meeting hers. "I want your insights on this. It's going to be our home, after all."

She seemed momentarily stunned by my words, and then a soft smile tugged at the corners of her lips. As we delved into the discussion with Jerry, I could see Sarah analyzing the floor plans intently.

"What do you think, Sarah?" I asked, genuinely eager to hear her thoughts. "Did you see anything that needs improvement or something you want to change or add?"

Her focus fell on the bathroom layout, and she furrowed her brow in thought. "There doesn't seem to be much storage in the kitchen and bathrooms, they need more cabinets and drawers. You might need additional storage space for toiletries and towels also."

"That's an excellent idea," I said, glad I brought her with me. "Jerry, make sure there's plenty of storage in the bathrooms and kitchen. You heard the lady. I want it to be as functional as it is beautiful."

"Absolutely, no problem." Jerry nodded, already scribbling notes on his pad.

We discussed more ideas and time frames for when it could be started and the completion time. I wanted it done as fast as possible and if that meant paying extra to get more people to build it, I had no problem with it.

After Jerry promised he would take care of everything and get the home started as soon as possible, we left to go back to the RV. I was excited about the new home and filled the drive home blathering about the new house. I was so busy talking that I didn't notice that Sarah hadn't said much until we were back in the RV.

"Sarah? What's wrong?" Had I screwed things up with her?

I could hear her breathing had increased and was worried that she might not want to live with me any longer. What if I had overstepped? What if she didn't want this kind of commitment? The fear gnawed at my insides, turning my excitement into a knot of worry. I stole glances at her, searching her eyes for a clue to what she was thinking.

My heart raced with every passing moment, my mind a whirlwind of uncertainty. Did she think I was moving too fast? Did she regret getting involved with me? My anxiety weighed on me like a ton of heavy stones.

I stole glances at her while we sat at the table, her presence was both comforting and unsettling. I wanted to ask, to know what she truly thought, but my tongue felt tied in knots. My mind raced with all the things I should have said, but nothing came out.

Sarah looked at me, her eyes were wide and her hands shaking. "What... exactly... did you mean when you said it was going to be **our** home?"

Our home. The phrase hung in the air, ripe with a new uncertainty I wasn't expecting. I wanted it to be a promise of our shared future. Yet, my fear of misreading her feelings held me back.

I swallowed hard. My throat was suddenly as dry as a desert. I could feel my heart racing as fear swirled within me. Trying to find the right words, I looked into her eyes, searching for any sign of what she might be feeling.

"Um... Well," I began softly speaking, "when I said, "our home," I meant it exactly like I said it. I thought, and tell me if I was wrong, that..." This was way more difficult than I thought it would be. "I thought that you and I... um... I can see a future with you. I want you in my life. I know so many things have gone wrong since we met, but you stayed, even if that wasn't your initial plan. If you don't feel the same, you need to tell me and stop me from making an even bigger fool of myself."

My palms were sweating, and the beat of my heart thudded in my ears. My gaze never left hers. I was taking the biggest chance of my life and I needed to know how she felt. "I care about you more than I ever thought I'd care about anybody. So please, tell me how you feel." My voice trembled slightly at the end, and I held my breath as I waited.

Sarah met my eyes with a depth of emotion that surprised me. For a moment, time seemed to freeze. Her eyes, those beautiful, caring eyes, softened with something akin to deep affection or maybe even love.

"Hudson," she began, her voice soft, "I care about you too. More than I expected, more than I know how to express." Her words washed over me like a gentle breeze. A rush of relief flooded my senses, and I felt like I could finally breathe. Her smile was tender, a genuine smile that reached her eyes.

Her response, filled with warmth and sincerity, lifted the weight off my shoulders. I felt a profound sense of gratitude and a surge of hope. Tears filled her eyes, but I could see they were tears of joy. Sarah embraced me, and she... felt like home.

・♥・♥・♥・♥・♥・

## Sarah

When Hudson and I woke up that morning, the world had transformed overnight. A blanket of pure white snow stretched as far as the eye could see and draped the landscape in a serene, winter wonderland. The sight took our breath away, and we shared a moment of quiet awe before the excitement of the day ahead kicked in.

We bundled up against the cold, our breaths visible in the crisp winter air, and loaded our vehicles with our belongings. The crunch of snow beneath our boots resonated in the stillness of the morning as we made our way further into Hudson's property.

As we arrived at our new home, a sense of anticipation and joy bubbled within me. This house, our house, stood proud against the snowy backdrop, promising warmth and comfort within its walls. Together, we unloaded our few belongings from the RV, the air filled with laughter and the sound of our voices echoing through the nearly empty house.

It wasn't long before the quiet of the morning was interrupted by the arrival of a delivery truck. Delivery men unloaded the furniture that would soon fill our home with cozy evenings, lazy mornings, intimate conversations, and shared dreams.

Hudson's phone rang. When he answered, he mouthed to me, "Attorney." While the conversation continued, his smile grew larger, and his eyes widened. The most he said was, "Uh, huh," "Okay, and finally "Thank you." One-sided conversations are the worst, but when he finally hung up, his eyes lit up with uncontainable happiness.

"The judge ruled on the gold. Guess who's going to get to keep it! And... Victoria finally told them where the coins were that she took!" Hudson was so excited that he was nearly shouting. Before I could even congratulate him, he swept me off my feet, twirling us around in sheer excitement as I hung on for dear life.

"Congratulations Sarah!" he whooped joyously.

I laughed at his words. "Why are you congratulating me? I should be congratulating you. You get to keep the gold and the coins. You can sell them if you want. Buy yourself something."

He looked at me with a wicked grin on his lips. "I don't need the gold to buy myself anything. I'm rich... remember? You on the other hand are the proud owner of the gold. I told my attorney to list you as the person who found it and gave my okay for you to keep all of it. You can do whatever you want to do. Keep it or sell it. It's your choice."

The shock of what he just said froze me. "Wha... w... what! No! It was found on your land. It should be yours!" I couldn't imagine what he was thinking.

His smile was tender, and his voice softened as he spoke, making my heart skip a beat. "Sarah, consider it a wedding present from me," he said blushing. "That is... if you'll have me. I love you and want to spend the rest of my life with you." He looked at me with pleading eyes.

The moment hung in the air; a pause filled with so much emotion. My eyes welled up with tears of joy, and I reached out to touch his face gently. "I love you too." I whispered, my voice quivering, "Yes!"

# The End

If you enjoyed this, you'll love **Unlikely Alliances.**

You can read it for free on Amazon Unlimited here.

**Ethan Blackwood** is a gorgeous, charming, and charismatic billionaire businessman with a reputation as intense as his expensive tailored suits.

**Olivia Hayes** is a tenacious private detective. She's sharp-witted, fiercely independent, and skilled in ways that could prove deadly. To look at her, you'd never guess she carries hidden scars.

In the heart of Crystal Springs, where secrets are as common as shadows, Olivia is about to have her world turned upside down when Ethan walks into her office. Their lives collide in a whirlwind of mystery, danger, passion and desire,

Olivia, with her fiery determination, is not one to be easily impressed. But Ethan is different. His allure is undeniable, even to someone who's sworn off men forever. As she delves into the case, she discovers secrets that could destroy the peace and security of the picturesque small town she calls home.

Ethan finds himself captivated by Olivia's fierce independence and keen intellect. She challenges him in ways no one ever has, and he can't help but be drawn to the intensity in her eyes. Yet, behind her strength, he sees a vulnerability like nothing he's witnessed before.

In a town where danger lurks in every corner and trust is a rare commodity, Olivia and Ethan must navigate a web of lies, deceit, and unspoken desires. As they work together to unravel a high-stakes case, they find themselves entangled in a complex game of temptation and betrayal.

Will they succumb to the undeniable chemistry between them, or will the shadows of doubt consume them? In a world where nothing is as it seems, Olivia must choose between holding onto the defenses that have saved her time and time again or surrendering to the sweet uncertainty of love. Ethan must choose between what's worked in the past or the possibility of what could be.

Prepare for a thrilling ride of suspense, unexpected twists, and passion, "Unlikely Alliances" will keep you on the edge of your seat, questioning everything and everyone, until the very last page.

Read **Unlikely Alliances** on Amazon here.

If you live in Australia, click here.

If you live in the United Kingdom, click here.

If you live in Canada, click here.

# Unlikely Alliances Sneak Peak

## Chapter One

Olivia

As I stood at the edge of Main Street, I gazed over the picturesque small town of Crystal Springs. Nestled among the majestic mountains of Colorado, it exuded a charm that was hard to resist. Neat rows of quaint shops lined the streets, their colorful facades created a welcoming atmosphere. A soft, cool breeze rustled through the leaves of towering pine trees, carrying with it a sense of tranquility.

The crisp morning air carried the refreshing clean scent of evergreens, mingling with the fragrance of fresh dew on the grass. The town looked like it was straight out of a picture postcard. The residents moved about with an air of contentment, their smiles masking the underlying secrets that I knew all too well.

But I knew better than to be fooled by the pristine façade. Crystal Springs held secrets; secrets known only to the town's wealthy residents who wielded their influence behind closed doors like a puppet master pulling the strings to control the narrative. The town's tranquility belied the hidden agendas that lay beneath the surface, waiting to be uncovered.

The wealthy residents, with their opulent lifestyles, held the strings of power and influence. Behind closed doors, alliances were forged, and deals were made, shaping the town's destiny. I sensed the simmering tension beneath the surface, a volatile mix of privilege and deceit.

I stepped into my small private detective office; a haven tucked away from the prying eyes of the town's elite. Leather-bound books, their pages holding the knowledge I had acquired over the years, filled the shelves. The aroma of worn leather and freshly brewed coffee mingled with the scent of ink and old paper, creating an inviting atmosphere that was all mine.

My desk was cluttered with case files, a reflection of my relentless pursuit of the truth. The walls were adorned with diplomas and commendations from my time in the military and the skills I honed during my service.

I took a moment to appreciate the worn leather chair that had become my trusted companion, as I settled into it, my gaze fell upon the evidence boards where I pinned newspaper clippings and photographs related to my current case. The headlines screamed of a high-profile art theft that rocked Crystal Springs.

I couldn't shake off the feeling that there was more to it than what met the eye. My gut instincts rarely led me astray, and they were urging me to dig deeper into the tangled web of secrets that inundated this town, even if I didn't currently have a client.

I'd seen firsthand the dark underbelly of the world during my time in the military. Now, as a private detective, it was my duty to protect those who couldn't protect themselves or didn't even know they needed protection. Crystal Springs' secrets and the town's influential residents didn't intimidate me. I'd seen and experienced worse. If anything, they fueled my determination to uncover the truth and bring justice to those who deserved it.

I traced the edge of a photograph with my fingers, my mind already racing with possible leads. I knew I couldn't do it alone, especially in a town where power and money spoke volumes. I would need allies, unlikely as they might be. I set my sights on collaborating with a mysterious billionaire, determined to expose the shadows that plagued the town.

But I refused to be intimidated by the powerful and influential residents who thought they were untouchable. In my office, I was the master of my domain.

My military background and expertise in self-defense and marksmanship lent a unique perspective to my work as a private investigator. The skills honed during my years of service molded me into a formidable force. No one made the mistake of doubting my skills more than once.

I'd earned a reputation for unwavering dedication to justice. Clients sought me out when they needed someone relentless and resourceful, unafraid to delve into the darkest corners to uncover the truth.

As I sifted through the latest batch of evidence, my suspicions about Ethan Blackwood, the billionaire, began to crystallize. The timing of his arrival in town, coupled with his rumored connections to influential figures, raised red flags in my mind. His calculated charm hid his true intentions lurking just beneath the surface.

I couldn't dismiss the idea that Ethan might be somehow involved in the recent crime that shook the town to its core. His immense wealth and notorious reputation as a bad boy only added fuel to my growing suspicions. But I knew better than to jump to conclusions. I would need concrete evidence before I could confront him.

With each new piece of information, my determination to expose the truth intensified. My instincts were now poking me, telling me to dig deeper and uncover the secrets that lay behind the charming smile of the billionaire. I would unravel the web of deception, no matter the obstacles I encountered along the way.

Rumors burned through the town like wildfire. It buzzed with whispers of Ethan Blackwood and his alleged involvement in the crime. While the evidence was circumstantial and slim at best, my gut instincts and intuition told me there was more to the story than met the eye.

Even in the face of skepticism, nothing was going to stop me from uncovering the truth. The town needed answers, and I was determined to unearth them, even if it meant challenging the status quo. Even if it meant making some very powerful people very uncomfortable.

Just as my mind delved deeper into my thoughts, the office door swung open. In walked Ethan Blackwood, wearing an expensive tailored suit. He exuded an undeniable aura of danger. He was tall and commanding, with an athletic physique that spoke of disciplined strength.

The second our eyes met; the air crackled with tension. I saw the shadows in his piercing gaze, mirroring my own determination. I knew this encounter would be far from ordinary. Our personalities would clash. It was inevitable.

I couldn't deny the striking features that held the power to captivate hearts. His dark, tousled hair hinted at a rebellious spirit, while a strong jawline accentuated his rugged masculinity. Yet, it was the confident swagger and the simmering intensity that truly set him apart from other men.

Our first exchange of words was akin to a verbal sparring match, filled with subtle jabs and defensive maneuvers. My sharp tongue matched his own, refusing to back down. Each sentence held an undercurrent of challenge, our verbal dance was a testament to the clash of our wills.

"You don't strike me as the type to take kindly to investigators poking around," I remarked, my voice laced with equal measures of skepticism and curiosity.

Ethan's lips curled into a knowing smile. "You don't strike me as the type to be easily deterred. But I warn you, Miss Hayes, curiosity can be a dangerous trait."

I narrowed my eyes. "Danger doesn't scare me, Mr. Blackwood. I've faced far worse."

Our banter continued; a spoken chess match where neither of us would concede ground. The more we sparred, the clearer it became that our paths were destined to intersect, our fates entwined in a game of shadows and secrets.

Our heated exchange escalated. We seemed to be determined to undermine the other's reputation and abilities. I oozed skepticism as I questioned Ethan's motives and involvement in the recent art theft of Jean-Pierre Bosqe, In This Way, a painting on loan from a collector, which sold for ninety-three million dollars at auction. He responded with an arrogant demeanor that only intensified our mutual animosity.

My skepticism was a product of years of investigative skills, both in the military and as a private detective. I'd seen through the disguises of many, and Ethan Blackwood would be no exception. I questioned his loyalty, his integrity, and his true intentions, refusing to let his wealth and charm cloud my judgment.

Ethan's confidence bordered on cockiness. He dismissed my doubts with a casual wave of his hand, believing his reputation and influence were enough to protect him from any scrutiny. He saw me as a mere inconvenience, an obstacle to overcome on his path to protecting his own interests.

His arrogance was beyond intolerable. Just because he was rich, he probably thought he deserved to be believed, that he deserved special dispensation to get and have whatever he wanted. He was being a pompous jerk, and I wasn't going to let him get away with it.

Our personalities crashed on every level, like two opposing forces destined to collide. I, methodical and calculated, believed in following the evidence and unraveling the truth. He, impulsive and driven by his own agenda, relied on his money and power to navigate through life. Our differing approaches to solving problems fueled the fires to such a degree that Niagara Falls wouldn't be able to put it out.

But I was determined, and I met Ethan's arrogance with unwavering resolve. "Don't underestimate me, Mr. Blackwood," I spat, my voice laced with defiance and caution. "I've taken down more formidable opponents than you. If you're hiding something, I'll find it. You can bet on that and mark my words, the truth will be revealed, no matter how hard you try to bury it." My warning hung in the air, a challenge that Ethan couldn't ignore. I threw down the gauntlet and I would uncover the secrets he held.

• ♥ • ♥ • ♥ • ♥ • ♥ •

## Ethan

Olivia stood her ground, her determination radiating from every fiber of her being. I couldn't help but notice a flicker of intrigue in her brown eyes. Masked beneath the layers of animosity, a hidden curiosity sparked. Her warning to not underestimate her rang loud and clear.

I'd encountered adversaries before, but there was something about Olivia that stirred my interest. Her expertise in investigation and military background intrigued me. Despite our initial clash, a grudging respect began to take root within me.

Her gaze was steady and resolute. She was smart and saw an opportunity to set aside our differences for the sake of the investigation. With a calm yet determined voice, she proposed a temporary alliance, her words laced with practicality.

"Listen, Mr. Blackwood," Olivia began, her tone surprisingly measured. "We may not see eye to eye, but it's clear we both have a stake in uncovering the truth. Let's set aside our personal grievances and work together, at least until we solve this case. We can't afford to let our differences hinder our progress."

In that fleeting moment, I recognized the potential strength of joining forces. Our unique skills and abilities would complement each other. As much as I despised the idea of needing anyone, the reality of the situation began to sink in. The secrets that overshadowed Crystal Springs were deeper than I'd anticipated, and her determination could prove to be invaluable.

I reluctantly acknowledged the need for an alliance. "Fine," I conceded cautiously. "We should work together, but make no mistake, I won't be holding your hand."

Olivia's eyes narrowed, a hint of a knowing smile touching her lips. "Don't worry, Mr. Blackwood. I don't need anyone to hold my hand. You on the other hand... you need to be prepared to face the consequences of the truth, no matter what I find."

She needed to know I wasn't wild about this either. I crossed my arms and stared at her through narrowed eyes. "Make no mistake, Olivia," — my voice dripping with disdain, — "I won't go easy on you. And don't think for a second that this alliance changes anything between us. It's purely for the sake of expediency. I want answers now!"

Our partnership was born out of necessity rather than mutual trust or friendship. Both of us understood the dangers we were about to embark on. Trust was a luxury we couldn't afford.

Exchanging a wary glance, an unspoken understanding passed between us. We'd reluctantly joined forces, knowing the secrets we would uncover could potentially shatter the idyllic veneer of this town forever.

Continue reading "Unlikely Alliances" on Amazon here.

If you live in Australia, click here.

If you live in the United Kingdom, click here.

If you live in Canada, click here.

Printed in Great Britain
by Amazon